D1179879

Pieces *from the* Past

Elizabeth Penney

CountrySampler®

CountrySamplerFiction.com

Library of Congress-in-Publication Data
Pieces from the Past / by Elizabeth Penney
p. cm.
I. Title
2016939775

CountrySamplerFiction.com
(800) 282-6643
Antique Shop Mysteries™
Series Creator: Shari Lohner
Series Editors: Jenny Baumgartner and Shari Lohner
Cover Illustrator: Bonnie Leick

10 11 12 13 14 | Printed in China | 9 8 7 6 5 4 3 2 1

1

"Can you believe it's snowing again?" Maggie Watson asked her plump tabby, Snickers, who sat beside her on the seat in the breakfast nook. Both of them stared out of the tall windows at the flakes covering the already-thick winter blanket on Sedgwick Manor's grounds.

In response, Snickers mewed and twitched his tail. Maggie had thought Vermont winters were bad, but so far, this Maine February took the prize. It had been snowing daily for weeks—sometimes a little, sometimes a lot—with very few breaks of sunshine. Although the mansion was large and spacious, she was definitely coming down with cabin fever.

Despite the weather, though, Maggie was enjoying living in the quaint fishing village and tourist destination of Somerset Harbor. She'd spent most of her adult life in Bennington, Vermont, but when her aunt, Evelyn Bradbury, had passed away suddenly and left her Sedgwick Manor and the Carriage House Antiques shop, she'd decided to make the move to Maine. She'd really had no reason not to make the change. A widow of three years, Maggie had also become an empty-nester after her daughter, Emily, had started college a few months ago. Her new life here allowed her to indulge her lifelong passions for antiques and history, passions she and her aunt had shared.

Maggie took another sip of coffee then set the mug aside and reached for her aunt's leather-bound journal. She'd found it shortly after her arrival at Sedgwick Manor and was gradually working her way through it. Her aunt had often said she felt a personal connection with the items she acquired, and the journal held her fascinating—and sometimes cryptic—observations.

"What should we read about today?" she said aloud. Beside her, Snickers responded by flopping onto his back, closing his eyes, and reaching out a paw to rest on Maggie's jeans-clad leg. She grinned and rubbed his belly, then leafed to where she had left off. The top of the page read *Secrets and Mysteries* and then, underneath it, *Second-Floor Storage Room.* She had been so busy settling in and learning the ropes at the antiques shop that Maggie had rarely ventured upstairs into the large bedroom. It had served as a storage room for as long as Maggie could remember. She'd peeked inside a couple of times, but the sheer amount of stuff crammed into the space had overwhelmed her. Maybe today was the day to venture in and investigate. She glanced at the regulator clock on the kitchen wall, wondering whether she should head to the shop instead. *Just before eight.* The shop didn't open until ten, and June would be there on time if not early.

Getting up from the bench, she grabbed the journal and her cell phone. Snickers opened his eyes and blinked in surprise at her sudden movements. "Come on, lazybones," she said. "We're going to uncover some secrets and mysteries."

Snickers at her heels, Maggie entered the front hall and climbed the curving grand staircase. As had become a habit, she stole an admiring glance at the Swarovski Austrian crystal chandelier hanging in the main entrance. Its light always made a stunning impression on the beautiful antiques below.

In the upstairs hall, she took a moment to cross over to where the gallery overlooked the huge, formal living room below. The scene looked like an aerial view of a fine-homes magazine spread. Even though Maggie had been a regular visitor to the manor as a child, she'd never dreamed she would own this spectacular house. She'd been here for several months now, but she was still getting used to the idea. Crossing the hall, Maggie went to the door of the storage room and opened it. She stepped inside and paused beside a lovely cherry secretary desk on her right. Maggie placed the journal and her cell phone on it and admired its elegant lines. Judging by the ball-and-claw feet, it looked to be eighteenth-century American Chippendale style. Maggie felt a touch of pride. Her ability to identify antiques was improving every day.

Turning to survey the room, she rested her hands on her hips and took a deep breath. Her plan was to take a look around, see if she could figure out what was where, and choose something intriguing for further research.

"Where should we start?"

Snickers looked up at her, then wove between her ankles and made his way over to one of the windows. He squeezed his body between a box and a chest where a spot of sunshine lit a small bit of floor space. After plopping himself down, he began to lick one front paw.

Maggie snorted. "You're a lot of help." Ignoring her, he moved on to groom a hind leg.

Her cell phone chirped. To Maggie's surprise, it was Emily. They usually only spoke on weekends. "Hi, honey. How are you?"

"Great. What are you up to?" Emily sounded like her usual chipper and happy self.

"I'm actually upstairs getting ready to check out the storage room." As she spoke, Maggie took a step farther into the room. Should she start from the doorway and work her way in? "Aunt Evelyn always said that some family heirlooms were in here."

"I hope so, considering what a mess it is," Emily laughed. "I couldn't believe how much stuff Aunt Evelyn managed to cram in there. Be careful; something might fall on you."

"Tell me about it." Maggie edged her way past a precariously balanced stack of crates. "I'm debating where to start," she said, working her way toward a clothing rack with colorful fabrics inside of clear garment bags.

"I'd pick something that looks cool and go from there."

"Good idea." She unzipped one large bag full of dresses that appeared to be from the 1920s and '30s. "Next time you're home, you should look at these flapper dresses I just found." She held up a red silk with copious amounts of fringe, noting its slim construction. "They'll probably fit you."

"Nice." Then Emily went silent, and Maggie's motherly instinct told her she had something on her mind. She waited in silence and flipped up the latch on a trunk. When she opened the lid, she saw marvelous 1800s ladies' undergarments—bloomers, petticoats, and corsets. Emily would get a kick out of those too.

"Mom," Emily finally said, "a guy in one of my classes, Ian, asked me on a date." Emily's heart had been badly bruised when her high school boyfriend broke up with her, although in theory she agreed it made sense because they were going to different colleges.

"Oh? Do you like him?" Maggie opened a shirt box and found it stuffed full of old-fashioned valentine cards. She felt a brief swell of emotions, sadness at the reminder of what had been a special holiday for her and Richard but also happiness at this unexpected evidence of love.

"I don't know. I mean, he seems nice. And he's cute. But I don't know if . . ."

"If you're ready."

"Exactly. I just don't want to lead him on, let him think I'm more interested than I am."

"But you want to go." At Emily's assent, Maggie paused to consider carefully what to tell her. She thought wistfully of the days when Emily's biggest problem had been getting her homework done on time or dealing with a mean classmate on the playground. Now she was seeking advice about matters of the heart, an area where Maggie felt woefully unequipped. She hadn't exactly dated a lot herself. Richard had been her one and only.

"Be honest," she finally said. "Tell him the truth—that you just got out of a serious relationship and you're not ready to rush into anything. But that said, you would be happy to spend time with him and let your friendship develop."

After a pause, Emily said, "Oh, Mom, that's perfect. Some of my friends were telling me to play hard to get. I'd rather be up front from the start." She heard Emily sigh with relief.

"Good thinking, sweetie." It warmed Maggie's heart that she and her daughter shared such a close bond. After more chitchat, Emily had to go and, with a promise to call at the regular time on Sunday, she hung up.

Maggie tucked the phone into her pocket, thrilled that her independent daughter had sought her advice. After the challenges of adolescence were made even more difficult by the loss of her father, Emily needed room to make her own decisions and choices.

Maggie's gaze fell on a gorgeous black-and-gold enamel box sitting next to a ladder-back rocking chair where Snickers had found a new perch. She had seen smaller ones used as jewelry boxes but never one this large. It had to be about a foot long and ten inches deep.

She hunkered down and ran her fingers gently over the top, admiring the quality of the artwork, an Asian motif of figures, pagodas, and trees. Had one of her Sedgwick seafaring ancestors brought this back from a voyage to the East? Maybe there was a fabulous treasure inside.

She tested the lid, hoping it wasn't locked, and was gratified when it opened readily, the lid squeaking as it rose. The smell of old cotton and lavender drifted to her nose, but to her disappointment, she saw the box only held what looked like a stack of fabric squares. Maybe a family member had made them. She reached inside and gently lifted them out one by one, noticing that each had a different design: a whale, three pine trees, a sailing ship, Old Faith Chapel. All the blocks depicted something related to Somerset Harbor."Look at this, Snickers." She held up a block. "Sedgwick Manor." He didn't seem to be impressed by the portrait of the mansion in cloth.

A night sky with stars and a crescent moon encircled the mansion. She flipped it over and saw writing on the back. The ink was faded and the writing old-fashioned, but she finally made out the signature. *Nellie Linton, 1898.*

Nellie Linton must have sewn the beautifully stitched piece. Was she related to Ina Linton, one of Maggie's friends in the historical society? She would have to ask. Maggie turned over the rest of the pieces—fourteen in all—and discovered that each had been signed with a different name but the same year.

She studied each carefully but was disappointed not to find one signed by a Sedgwick. Maybe she had stumbled on one of the mysteries her aunt had written about. A trickle of excitement ran down her spine. She made her way back to the secretary desk and picked up the journal. Turning to the section she'd been in previously, she scanned more pages until she found an entry under 1898. It mentioned a quilt.

Friendship quilt, the entry read. Maggie had never heard of a friendship quilt and guessed the names on the backs of the squares were the friends. Who were they? She needed to do some research. Her friend Fran Vosburg owned The Quilt Cupboard downtown. She would be able to help. Fran's shop sold quilting supplies and handmade quilts and even held quilting lessons.

Maggie looked at the rest of the entry. It included a note and a quote.

> *14 blocks, various Somerset Harbor scenes.*
> *Sometimes being a friend means keeping a secret.*
>
> *The human heart has hidden treasures, in secret kept,*
> *in silence sealed* — *Charlotte Brontë*
>
> *1898.*

Maggie didn't know a lot about her ancestors, but her great-grandmother Julia Sedgwick had lived at Sedgwick Manor then.

What was the secret that caused Julia to tuck away the makings of this friendship quilt so long ago?

2

Maggie placed the quilt blocks back in the enamel box and gently closed the lid. She would take it over to Fran's shop this afternoon. Glancing at her phone, she saw it was almost ten. June would be opening the shop soon, so she coaxed Snickers out of the room and downstairs to the kitchen with her.

She glanced out of the window. The short footpath across the grounds to Carriage House Antiques was buried in snow.

These days, she either drove or walked along the road to the shop. At twenty degrees, she'd take the car today, thank you very much. After putting on her coat and boots, she strode to the door but stopped when, out of the window, she saw that the driveway hadn't been plowed yet. That was odd. Aunt Evelyn's faithful landscaper, Nate Gregory, had recently added snowplowing to the many services he offered, and he was always very reliable. She pulled out her cell phone and gave him a call.

He answered right away. "Hey, Maggie. I'm sorry. The pickup truck broke down. I'm at the garage now and it should be good to go in half an hour."

Half an hour. Should she wait or . . . ? Inspiration struck as she remembered something she had seen hanging in the laundry room. "That'll be fine, Nate. Get to it when you can. Thanks." She would shovel the steps herself first, though, because walking out there would pack the snow, causing ice to form.

A few minutes later, bundled in boots, parka, hat, and gloves, Maggie began shoveling the steps outside the breakfast nook, feeling virtuous about getting out in the fresh—if cold—air. Her husband had been an avid skier, and he'd always told her that

13

brisk outdoor activity was a cure for the winter blues. She usually filed this advice in the back of her mind, preferring to cuddle up with Snickers in front of a cozy fire, a mystery novel in hand.

A faint mew penetrated her thoughts, and she turned to see Snickers sitting on the other side of the French door, peering out at her. She thrust the shovel into a snowbank and then opened the door just wide enough for her furry friend.

"Come on out. It's good for you, I promise." She said it to herself as much as to him. She was already missing the snugness of the quilt on her bed.

He gave her a suspicious stare then slipped through the opening with mincing steps. Although Snickers loved being outdoors three seasons of the year, he rarely went out when that nasty white stuff was piled high.

While Snickers watched from the cleared steps, Maggie shoveled the footpath. The snow was light and fluffy, like old-fashioned soap flakes. It reminded her of an article in one of Aunt Evelyn's magazines that described how soap flakes could be used to make fake decorative snow for displays. Living in the manor was like an immersion course in antiques and collectibles.

Glancing back at Snickers, she saw he was batting at a lone brown leaf on a bush by the steps. It floated down to the snow below. After hesitating a second or two, his instinct took over, and he pounced on it. Maggie gave a hoot of laughter at the look of alarm on his face after suddenly finding himself buried in snow up to his whiskers,.

"Didn't really think that through, did you?" Still chuckling, she plucked him from the drift and carried him inside to the laundry room. She sat him on the washing machine and dried him off with an old towel. When she was finished, she spied a pair of snowshoes hanging from a peg next to the rain slickers and jackets Aunt Evelyn had used. *It wouldn't take more than a few minutes to snowshoe over to the store. Much quicker than walking along the road or shoveling all the way down the path.*

She strapped on the shoes and trudged over to the shop, not anticipating the intense workout snowshoeing required. When she finally entered the shop, she was puffing and sweating and had sworn off any more snowshoeing—ever.

"What happened to you?" June asked in a surprised tone.

Maggie pulled off her boots and unzipped her coat. "I had the bright idea to snowshoe over instead of walking or taking the car. I'll never do that again." The very tiring and undignified waddle she'd had to use to move through the drifts had been a lesson in humility. She tugged at the wet leg of her jeans. "They kept falling off, so I went in up to my knee."

"You should get a pair of modern snowshoes. They're much easier to maneuver." June was clearly trying to keep a straight face. When Maggie met her eye, she became suddenly engrossed in straightening a crocheted doily on the arm of the sofa. "I'll ask Kurt for a recommendation," she said, her back to Maggie. Kurt was June's husband of over twenty-five years.

"No thanks. My snowshoeing days are over. And I don't need anyone else to know that this *ever* happened." Maggie slipped on the pair of moccasins she kept at the store. Then she realized something: She had to get back to the house after work. "Think you can give me a ride home?"

June adjusted the position of a crystal lamp on an end table next to a red velvet sofa. "Of course."

Maggie padded over to the display June was putting together. She studied the sofa and matching chair, marble coffee table topped with clear crystal and red glass boxes, and the standing lamp with a beaded lampshade. Maggie appreciated June's talent for decorating with antiques. After a decade of managing the shop, she had quite an eye for it.

Aunt Evelyn had always grouped the merchandise in roomlike settings, an attractive and effective approach Maggie and June still used. Maggie said, "Valentine's Day never looked so good."

June stood back and studied the display of red-and-white accents that highlighted the holiday setting. "It's not too much?"

Maggie shook her head. She examined the intricate beading on the lampshade. She remembered the special traditions she and Richard had shared on this holiday: the bouquet of red roses, one bloom for each year of marriage; the intimate dinner at their favorite Italian restaurant; another funny yet sentimental card she would tuck away in a shoe box. Returning her attention to the lampshade's swirling design, she asked, "What period is this? It's gorgeous."

"Art deco. I love it too." June picked up a red-and-white trinket box shaped like a heart. "And here's another art deco item. See the silver heart design woven through the top?"

Maggie took the box and examined it. "Very nice." She set it down and admired the display. "I'll bet you sell everything here. What you've done is so charming."

"Thanks. I sure hope so. But if we do sell everything, you know what that means? We'll have to find more stock."

Maggie's pulse beat a little faster. "I hope I'm ready." Since Maggie had moved to Somerset Harbor, June had been coaching and instructing her on how to identify and choose the best pieces. They'd traveled together to estate sales, private sales, shows, and other dealers to make selections. She'd recently told Maggie it was about time for her to step out and make some purchases on her own.

"I do. In fact—" The shop telephone rang. "Hold that thought," June said apologetically. She hurried to the counter and answered the phone. "Carriage House Antiques. Oh, hi, Ruth!"

Ruth Harper was a friend and the president of the local historical society.

"Hold on," June said. "Let me put you on speakerphone. I want Maggie to hear this." June pushed a button on the phone and gestured for Maggie to join her.

"What's going on?" Maggie asked.

"You'll see." June raised her voice. "Ruth, can you hear me?"

"Loud and clear, June."

"Hi, Ruth," Maggie called, feeling slightly foolish as she always did when on speakerphone. It was like yelling into an empty well.

"Maggie. I'm glad you're there. I was going to call you next." Ruth paused; whether for air or maximum impact, Maggie wasn't sure. "The Somerset lighthouse is going on the auction block."

"What?" June grabbed Maggie's arm. "The government is selling our lighthouse?"

Maggie was bewildered. "They sell lighthouses? I didn't know that." As far as she knew, they were a permanent part of the country's infrastructure, like highways and bridges.

"Yes," June said grimly. "All up and down the coasts, the government has been selling off lighthouses to the highest bidder. It's unconscionable. They're part of our heritage."

"Hold on, June," Ruth said. "It's not quite that bad." They heard her shuffling papers. "When I heard about it, I contacted them on behalf of the society. They sent me a pile of information. Let me see . . ."

Maggie and June exchanged impatient and nervous glances while they waited for Ruth to fill them in.

"Here it is." Ruth cleared her throat. "There is a special exception for preservationist groups. If we can prove that we can afford to make any currently needed repairs and then can maintain its upkeep, they will sign the lighthouse over to us for free."

"We'll have to find a way to afford it," June said. "We need to make sure it's preserved for future generations. Plus, it's a big tourist draw."

"I can understand that," Maggie said. "And a private owner might close off access." She hadn't been to the lighthouse yet, but she'd driven by the tall, white tower, majestic on its cliff-top perch overlooking the ocean. Almost nothing felt more like Maine than a pretty lighthouse.

"That's exactly right," Ruth said. "You're a quick study, just like your aunt. She always could figure out the core of a problem in no time flat."

Maggie felt a swell of pride at being compared to the aunt she had adored. "So what's the next step?"

"We need to figure out how to raise the funds," Ruth said. "Unfortunately, we may be talking tens of thousands, if not more. It has been sitting for decades without any TLC. I'll put it on the agenda for tonight's meeting."

June's eyes widened in dismay. "How on earth are we ever going to come up with that much money?"

Maggie had no idea, but she prayed inspiration would strike. The society had to save the lighthouse somehow.

When June dropped Maggie off at home at lunchtime, she saw that Nate had come and gone, leaving the drive clear. He had even removed the snow from her car—a reminder of the kindness that pervaded in Somerset Harbor.

Inside, she decided to make a grilled cheese sandwich and tomato soup for lunch, a winter favorite of Emily's and her own.

After lunch, which included Snickers enjoying a tidbit of cheese, Maggie loaded the Asian-inspired box she'd found that morning into the backseat of the car and drove to town. The flurries had stopped for the moment, and sunlight was breaking through the clouds, making the snow sparkle. *How pretty.* With their decorative lights and creative window displays, the brick and clapboard storefronts looked like a postcard of a picture-perfect coastal village in winter.

On an impulse, Maggie pulled into the parking lot of The Busy Bean, the coffee shop owned by Daisy Carter, a statuesque Southern belle with big hair and an even bigger personality. After being basically cooped up for days, Maggie felt like being social, and Daisy's place fit the bill.

The coffee shop resounded with chatter, laughter, and the clatter of dishes. Maggie didn't see Daisy anywhere, but her favorite table by the window was open, and she grabbed it. She took off her hat, gloves, and coat; Daisy's history in Georgia meant her shop was plenty warm, even in the most frigid weather.

As Maggie enjoyed the view of the quiet harbor, a petite young woman with spiky black hair and a charming grin hurried over. "Welcome to The Busy Bean. My name's Mackenzie. What can I get you?"

"Hi, Mackenzie. I'm Maggie." She skimmed the list of seasonal coffee drinks presented in a standing holder. "How about a Snowcap Mocha?" Although her coffee tastes were rather basic, she branched out every so often, thanks to Daisy's influence.

"Good choice." Mackenzie nodded. "I'll be right back." She bustled back to the counter and gave the order to Jenny, the waitress who had worked at The Bean for several years. Jenny started making the drink. Then Mackenzie buzzed over to the other side of the room to wait on a good-looking blond man sitting at another table. Unlike the other casually dressed patrons, he wore a suit and tie.

The bells over the door jingled, interrupting Maggie's thoughts. She saw Ina Linton tramp in, bundled up in a puffy blue parka and matching hat with a huge pompom. The elderly Ina was known for her striking—some would say strange—outfits. Maggie caught Ina's eye and waved for her to join her.

"Did you hear the news?" Ina said without preamble. "The feds are going to deep-six the lighthouse." After hanging up her coat and pulling off her hat, which left her fine white hair standing on end, she pulled back the chair and plopped down.

"Not totally, I hope," Maggie protested. "It'll still operate, won't it?"

Ina snorted. "So they say. But if we don't get it, who knows what'll happen? Some flatlander is likely to put in condos." Putting in condos was about the worst thing most Somerset Harbor residents could think of when it came to changes in property.

"That would be awful," Maggie agreed, although she doubted the structure could hold more than one or two dwellings. But if enough land came with the lighthouse, then condos were a real possibility.

Mackenzie brought Maggie's drink over. Maggie hummed appreciatively at the warm mug topped with whipped cream as Mackenzie took Ina's order—"coffee, black, no extras"—and scooted off again.

"She's new," Ina said, watching Mackenzie as she swung back to the counter and picked up the blond man's order. Lowering her voice, she whispered, "And I see that scoundrel Tyler Monroe is back in town."

"You mean the man Mackenzie is waiting on?" Maggie studied his chiseled face, groomed hair, and economical but elegant movements. His blue eyes twinkled at the waitress, making him seem approachable and pleasant. "He doesn't look like a scoundrel."

Her companion scowled. "Looks can be deceiving. Tyler is no friend of Somerset Harbor or our historical properties."

"Condos?" Maggie guessed.

"Gas station. Decimated the Perkins farm up on Route 1."

"That's too bad."

Mackenzie appeared with Ina's coffee. "New in town?" the older woman asked her.

"Yes, I am," Mackenzie replied politely. "I'm here to find out some information about my great-great-grandparents, Sarah and John Floyd. They used to live here."

"When was that, dear?" Ina's ears perked up. She loved to share her knowledge and help people. "I've lived here all my life, so maybe I knew them."

Mackenzie gave a tinkling little giggle. "Oh, about a hundred years ago. I don't think you knew them."

Ina scrunched up the right side of her mouth. "I'm not *that* old." Then she squinted at the waitress over the rim of her coffee mug. "Why don't you come to the historical society meeting tonight? Maybe we have information about them in our museum."

"I'd love that. When and where?"

Ina filled her in, and Mackenzie dashed off. "I do love to recruit young blood," Ina said. "We need it desperately, or in a few years, our society will die off."

"I'm not *that* old," Maggie protested, grinning at Ina. "I hope I have a few good decades left. Fran too."

"Of course. I was talking about the rest of us geezers."

The door bells jingled again and James Bennett, the handsome alderman and preservationist, entered the coffee shop. Maggie tried to ignore the tiny flutter she felt when she saw him. James sometimes worked for the Carriage House, repairing and restoring furniture, and since she had been in town, they had developed a very pleasant friendship.

Ina waved her arm frantically at James and yelled, "James! Over here!" Naturally everyone in the shop turned to look at who was making so much noise, and Maggie shrank back in her seat. She loved Ina, but the older woman could be embarrassing if you were easily discomfited or hated attention.

James made a beeline for their table. Tall, with dark hair and blue-gray eyes, he resembled a catalog model in his gray peacoat and navy corduroys.

"Good afternoon, ladies," he said. His gaze lingered on Maggie's face. "I'd like to speak with you when you have a moment."

3

"Can it wait a minute?" Ina's tone was insistent. "We have an emergency here."

James gave Maggie an amused glance. "What's that, Ina?"

"The lighthouse is for sale, and we need you to help us stop the feds from making a huge mistake."

He held up a hand. "Hold on, Ina. What are you talking about?" He pulled up a chair. "What's this about the lighthouse?"

Ina and Maggie filled him in, taking turns to explain the situation. "You understand I don't have jurisdiction over the federal government, right?" he asked when they'd finished. "I mean, I'm just a town alderman."

The older woman pursed her lips. "I get that. But maybe you could put some sand in the wheels if some city slicker tries to get town approval for a project."

"Like condos," Maggie put in.

His brows furrowed. "I'm sympathetic to your point, ladies. But if someone does their homework and their proposal is legal by town and state statutes and regulations, I—we—can't say no."

Ina hit the flat of her hand on the table. "I told people we needed something to protect that lighthouse and some of our other historic buildings. Everyone thought that would be too restrictive." She snorted. "Now they'll see."

"Wait, when was that?" Maggie asked.

"An ordinance regarding a historic district was voted down during a town meeting a couple of years ago," James said.

"Right after the Perkins farm went bye-bye." Ina shook her head. "Talk about a warning shot across the bow."

"I tell you what," James said. "I'll do all I can to help you raise funds so the society can take over the lighthouse. And if the town government can do something, you have my word it will."

"That will have to do, I suppose," Ina grumbled.

"I think it's a fabulous offer. Thanks, James," Maggie said, admiring him for upholding the legal side of his job and not letting his personal feelings influence his actions. "What was it you wanted to talk to me about?"

To her surprise, James shifted in his chair, his eyes darting around the room. "Can I call you later? I don't want to be late for an appointment." Leaving a few bills on the table for the check, he put on his coat and strode out of the coffee shop.

"He took off like a cat with a tin can tied to his tail." Ina's face was bemused. "I wonder what that was all about?"

Maggie wondered about that too. Oh well, she would have to wait for him to call. She decided to change the subject. "Ina, do you have an ancestor named Nellie Linton?"

"Why yes, I do. She was my grandmother. How did you know that?" Ina held her cup up to the pot Mackenzie held. Regular coffee came with refills, one reason the frugal Ina chose it. "Thank you, dear."

"I found a quilt square signed by her, along with a whole box of signed blocks from 1898. I want to see if Fran can give me any background on friendship quilts. That's what Evelyn called it."

"A friendship quilt. That sounds intriguing. Like a scrapbook in cloth."

After finishing their drinks, Maggie and Ina retrieved the Asian box from Maggie's car and darted the short distance to The Quilt Cupboard, eager to get to its warmth.

Fran Vosburg was arranging bolts of colorful fabric along the wall. She looked up and smiled when she saw them. After shoving an obstinate bolt into place, she strolled across to greet them.

"How are you two doing today? I was happy to see that the sun is finally shining." Slender and pretty, Fran had a girlish air and a sweet, shy nature.

"Me too," Ina said. "I was starting to feel like a hibernating bear." Once again, she pulled off her hat, leaving her hair sticking up in a tuft.

Maggie set the box on a long worktable. "I found some signed quilt blocks in the storage room today, and I wanted to see if you had any insights to give me." She gestured for Fran to open the box.

Fran lifted the lid and looked down at the contents. "Do you know how old they are?"

"They're from 1898. That's what the date says on the back of them. And Aunt Evelyn's journal said the same."

"My grandmother's name is on one of them," Ina added.

Fran reached into the pocket of her denim skirt and pulled out a pair of white cotton gloves. "Skin oils are bad for antique fabrics," she explained. She gently pulled out the pile and then laid the blocks, designs up, in three rows.

"The designs are related to Somerset Harbor," Ina noted aloud. She pointed out how each one related to the town. "Which one is Granny's?"

Maggie pointed to the one picturing Sedgwick Manor. Fran turned it over, then proceeded to turn over the rest of the blocks so they could study the signatures.

Ina peered closely at Nellie's writing. "Granny was quite a gal, you know," she announced. "She studied astronomy, on her own of course, since there wasn't much emphasis on girls' academic pursuits. We still have her telescope at the house."

Maggie's eyes met Fran's; they had both just figured out where Ina got her inquisitive nature. Maggie could imagine a lady who looked a lot like Ina studying the night sky and snooping on her neighbors with her spyglass.

"Evelyn has this listed as a friendship quilt in her journal," Maggie said. "Do you know much about those, Fran?"

Fran slid a block an inch to the right so that it was perfectly aligned with the others. "As it happens, I do. They were a fad in the 1800s. Women made them before a wedding, or before going West as pioneers, or just as family heirlooms."

"That must have been a nice memento for settlers who left their homes," Ina said.

"This particular example is really an album quilt because of the different images on each block. Friendship quilts often used the same block for each square, like the chimney sweep pattern." Fran rearranged the blocks, leaving a space in the center. "There's a block missing. A slightly larger one."

Maggie felt a thrill of excitement. "I wondered why there wasn't one with my great-grandmother's name, Julia Sedgwick. I found this box in the family storage room, so I know it has meaning for the Sedgwicks."

Ina peered into the box as if hoping it held something they had overlooked. "I wonder where the other block went."

"I have no idea," Maggie said. "But this quilt has a mysterious history. The journal said, *Sometimes being a friend means keeping a secret.*"

"Intriguing." Fran's eyes brightened at this quilt-related puzzle. "Why don't you bring these to the meeting tonight? Maybe we can help you solve the mystery of the missing quilt block."

Ina winked. "And figure out the secret. I do love secrets."

Outside the shop, Maggie asked Ina if she wanted a ride home. The elderly woman didn't own a car, and although she said walking kept her healthy, she wasn't averse to a ride now and then.

"Maybe I'll take you up on that." Ina scanned both ways for a break in traffic. "I need to get ready for our meeting tonight, and that will give me more time."

They had stepped through an opening in the snowbank and were about to cross the street when Ina grabbed Maggie's arm.

"Isn't that Mackenzie over there?" She pointed to an alley a couple of storefronts down from the quilt shop.

Maggie craned her head to see where Ina was pointing. A young woman was standing close to a young man dressed in a wool cap and an Army jacket. After a moment, she saw it was indeed the waitress from The Busy Bean, dressed for the outdoors in a black wool coat and matching gloves and beret. As Maggie watched in horror, the much larger man grabbed the diminutive waitress by the shoulders and shook her.

4

Before Maggie could react, Ina shouted, "Hey you!" and took off toward the couple, waving her arms wildly. Gathering her wits, Maggie clutched the box more tightly and followed, her heart beginning to pound.

What was he doing to Mackenzie? And what would he do when accosted by an elderly lady?

"Stop that! Let her go!" Ina shouted.

The man spotted them, and his eyes widened. Ina was bearing down on him, windmilling her arms. He released Mackenzie and backed away. Then he ran down the alley, turned at the end of it, and disappeared.

Ina put both hands on her hips and scowled in the direction he had fled. "Good thing he ran. I was going to beat the tar out of him."

"Are you all right?" Maggie asked Mackenzie, who was staring at Ina in amazement.

"I'm fine, thanks to you guys." She shook her head. "I can't believe you chased him away like that. Wow."

"Who was that guy anyway?" Ina demanded. "We should call the police and have him booked for assault."

Dismay flitted across Mackenzie's face. She put a hand on Ina's arm. "Please don't. He didn't mean anything by it."

Maggie had heard that women were often reluctant to press charges against abusive partners. "Who is he?" she asked gently, hoping Mackenzie would tell them more. "I don't think I've seen him around."

Mackenzie began to cry, wiping the tears away with one

gloved finger. "His name is Cody Becker. He's my ex-boyfriend. I can't believe he followed me here from Boston."

"Is that where you moved from?" Maggie asked.

The young waitress nodded, blowing her nose into the handkerchief Ina had handed her. "I just got here about a week ago. I was lucky to find a job right away, thanks to Jenny. We're old friends from church." She glanced over at The Busy Bean. "I'd better get back to work. My break is over."

Maggie and Ina accompanied Mackenzie across the street. "Where are you staying?" Maggie asked. *What if Cody catches her on the way home?*

"With Jenny." Mackenzie seemed to guess Maggie's concern and gave her a crooked smile. "Don't worry. I'll go home when she does."

Ina patted the young woman's arm at the front door of the coffee shop. "If you need anything, just call. Ina Linton. I'm in the book."

"Feel free to call me too. I'm Maggie Watson." Giving the box to Ina to hold, Maggie dug a Carriage House Antiques business card out of her purse, jotted her cell number on it, and gave it to Mackenzie.

Mackenzie tucked away the card, giving them one of her charming grins. "Thanks so much, Ina, Maggie. I guess what they say about small towns is true. People *are* nice." With that, she opened the door and disappeared inside.

After dropping Ina off, Maggie headed for home, looking forward to relaxing for a while before the historical society meeting. But when she unlocked the door, she was greeted by an indignant and yowling Snickers.

Setting her purse and the box on the hall table, she hunkered down to give her faithful companion a thorough petting. "Did you miss me?" She scratched under his chin and he purred in ecstasy. "I'll take that as a yes." When she stood and started for the kitchen, he bolted ahead of her. She laughed. "Or did you just require service?"

After giving him kibble and a little wet food, she opened the refrigerator, trying to decide what to have for dinner. Cooking for one—and eating alone—was often unappealing. Fond memories of family meals from Emily's childhood flitted through her mind as she pulled out a leftover eggplant Parmesan. She was lucky to have such experiences to cherish.

She covered the bowl with a paper towel and started the microwave, then rummaged for the leftover Caesar salad she'd made.

Her cell phone rang from the hall where she had left it. She dashed for it, thinking it might be Emily again.

The display read, *James Bennett*. He probably had a project for Carriage House Antiques he wanted to discuss.

"Hi, James. How are you?" Maggie started walking back toward the kitchen.

"I'm great. How about you?"

"I'm fine, just in the middle of making dinner before I go to the historical society meeting."

"If it's not a good time to talk—"

Maggie pulled the bowl out of the microwave with a mitt, holding the phone to her ear with her shoulder. "No, it's fine. I'm just microwaving leftovers. Go ahead."

"Well, I was wondering . . . I wanted to ask if you . . ."

She set the hot bowl on the table and retrieved the salad. "Come on, spit it out." She laughed to let him know she was teasing.

"Will you go with me to the Valentine's Day dinner at the Oceanview?" He spoke so fast the words almost blurred together.

Before she could think, Maggie found herself saying, "Yes, I'd love to." They talked for a few more minutes before he excused himself so that she could eat.

Through her meal, Maggie's mind was occupied by James's invitation. Even as she drove down to the historical society meeting, she questioned herself. Why hadn't she stalled by telling him she needed to think about it or had to check her calendar? Of course, it wasn't like she had a lot of competing engagements on Valentine's Day.

She was now in the same uncomfortable position that Emily had described to her earlier that day. Maggie wanted to go, but she was far from ready to get involved.

She found parking along Broad Street near the Queen Anne–style Victorian house where the society held its meetings. Every time she entered the building, she felt a rush of pleasure at the pretty building's rose, teal, and white color scheme.

Inside was just as pretty, with lots of woodwork, polished floors, and a gently ticking grandfather clock in the hall. The scents of lemon polish and brewing coffee wafted to her nose as she hung her coat on a peg. She walked to the meeting room where the usual members of the society were already gathered, chatting as they sipped on cups of coffee and munched on treats from The Busy Bean. After setting the box with the quilt squares on a side table, she placed a couple of spiced chocolate chip cookies, one of Daisy's new and addictive recipes, on her napkin and poured herself a hot cup of coffee.

Then she made her way to an empty seat among rows of wooden folding chairs. To her far left, she noticed a stranger in their midst, a good-looking man in his midtwenties. By the pad of paper and pen he held, she guessed he was from the newspaper. Maybe he was covering the lighthouse situation.

President Ruth Harper ambled to the front of the room and beamed at them. "Are we ready to get started, everyone?"

The others shifted in their seats, quieting their conversations. Ruth nodded at the young man. "First, I'd like to introduce our guest. Adrian Diaz is *The Herald*'s newest reporter. He's going to cover the lighthouse story." Adrian grinned and gave a small wave.

Ruth picked up an envelope from her pile of meeting paperwork and removed a letter. "The society has received this letter from the U.S. General Services Administration." She straightened the page and read the contents aloud. The GSA apologized that the historical society had been overlooked in the first round of the process, when the Department of Interior's National Park Services had searched for a public body or nonprofit organization to serve as steward of the lighthouse. Now the Somerset Harbor Lighthouse was being offered to them, subject to an application process and approval.

"The government will give it to us," Ruth explained, "if we can pay for repairs and regular upkeep. And unfortunately, repairs might be quite extensive—it's been a long time since the lighthouse was properly maintained by someone." She waved another piece of paper. "They recommend checking out the foundation and brickwork before taking it on."

Liz Young raised her hand. "What happens if we can't raise enough money?" A practicing psychologist, Liz was married to the pastor of Old Faith Chapel, the church Maggie attended.

Ruth's lips tightened into a thin line. "Then they'll auction it off to the highest bidder."

Ina bolted to her feet. "And we know what that means." She paused dramatically. "*Condos.*" She plopped back down as everyone began speaking at once, expressing concern and outrage. Maggie saw Adrian hide a grin at Ina's enthusiastic outburst. He jotted on his notepad.

Ruth banged the gavel, a rare event that startled everyone into silence. "I know this situation is of grave concern to us, and"—she nodded at Adrian—"it will be to the rest of the thinking population of Somerset Harbor. So I propose we come up with solutions. Any ideas?"

Daisy jumped in. "We need to ask people for donations. I can put out a bucket at The Busy Bean."

"Good idea, Daisy. We should also do a direct mail campaign and personal visits to wealthy residents," Liz said.

Fran added quietly, "We could hold some fundraisers too."

"And sell lighthouse-related items. We can put them in Carriage House Antiques, right, Maggie?" June said.

Maggie nodded. She wracked her brain for something to contribute. A thought came to mind. She waved her hand. "I think the first step is to assess the lighthouse and see exactly how much money we need."

"Good point, Maggie," Ruth said.

"James Bennett might be able to help us. He evaluates old buildings to determine how to preserve them. I would think he'd know what steps we need to take or could point us in the right direction."

"Yes, James will know what to do," affirmed Deborah Bennett, James's mother. She had recently started attending historical society meetings at Maggie's suggestion after many years as a recluse.

"He's perfect." Daisy nodded so hard in agreement that her hair bobbed too. "He's not only a professional, but he just adores the lighthouse."

The comments came fast and furious.

"We all love the lighthouse."

"It's a landmark."

"We need to preserve it."

Then Ina's voice was heard again. She spoke in a mysterious tone over the others. "It's also the site of one of the biggest tragedies in our town's history." She rose to her feet, holding up her hand until everyone stopped talking. "A young woman died there, over a century ago."

5

Just as Ina began to share the story, Mackenzie, the young waitress from The Busy Bean, entered the room. Maggie saw her look around at the rapt audience before slipping into a chair at the back. She quietly shrugged off her coat. Maggie was glad to see her, both because she was participating in the society and because she appeared to be all right. She'd been worried about the young woman since the shocking scene earlier that day with her ex-boyfriend.

Ina nodded at Mackenzie then went on. "Sarah Monroe was the daughter of one of Somerset Harbor's richest and most respected men, Horace Monroe."

Maggie startled at the name Monroe. The man Ina had pointed out at The Busy Bean. Was Tyler Monroe a descendant of Horace?

Ina continued. "They lived in Monroe Mansion, high on a cliff near the Somerset Lighthouse. Sarah often spent her time at the lighthouse, painting watercolors or just sitting on the rocks, watching the sea."

"When was this?" Daisy asked.

Ina held up her hand. "Hold on. I'm getting to that. Horace wanted Sarah to marry a much older banker in town, a man not known for his honesty."

Everyone made a sympathetic sound. Adrian was scribbling furiously on his notepad.

"Sarah, of course, objected to the marriage, and for good reason. It turns out the man was an embezzler, but no one knew it then. Rumor had it that Sarah loved another. But her pleas were to no avail. The wedding date was set." Ina paused.

"Go on, don't leave us hanging like that," Liz urged. "What happened?"

Ina lowered her voice. "In February 1898, on a cold, cruel winter day, Sarah's scarf was found at the foot of the lighthouse." She pointed dramatically to a case in the rear that contained several artifacts from the town's history. "That piece of scarf we have in the display and a note to her father were the only traces of Sarah ever found. To this day, most people believe that she killed herself. Others believe she ran away."

Following Ina's lead, the group rose and went to the back of the room. Part of a pink chiffon scarf embroidered with flowers lay in the case. "This scarf belonged to the missing heiress," Ina all but whispered.

Maggie imagined a young woman in Victorian dress wearing the scarf as she sat painting on the shore near the lighthouse.

"Can I get a picture?" the reporter asked. "I want to do a story on Sarah Monroe."

Several women murmured their approval. Ruth added, "I'll take the scarf out later so you can get a good shot of it."

Maggie's pulse leaped with excitement. "Ina, you said 1898. That's the same date as my friendship quilt."

"That's right," Fran said, snapping her fingers. "The back of the quilt blocks!"

"Friendship quilt?" Ruth sounded puzzled.

Maggie trotted across the room to her box. "I found these today, up in the storage room at Sedgwick Manor. I was planning to show them to you all once we finished our other business." She pulled out the blocks and displayed them to the others. "See? They're all signed with names and the year 1898. For some reason, they were never sewn together."

"One says *Sarah Monroe*," June said, pointing. "Did the missing heiress make that one, do you think?"

"I'll bet she did," Ina said. "I can't believe I didn't notice her name earlier."

"We didn't examine all the blocks closely," Maggie pointed out. She laid them out on the long table in rows, facedown to display the names and dates.

"I know that one." Deborah Bennett pointed to a square. "Priscilla Byrd Allen was my grandmother. My mother, Sarah Allen Keene, would probably have been a child when Priscilla did this block. It's wonderful to see her handiwork. James and I don't have any other quilts made by her. Or anything else for that matter."

"My grandmother did this one," Ina said. "Nellie Linton."

"This is great," Liz said. "A record of the past in cloth." She sighed in admiration. "And what fine work they did. You can barely see the stitches."

Then Mackenzie piped up. "There are three others named Sarah," she said in excitement. "Sarah Monroe, Sarah Jane Mackenzie, and Sarah Anne Stewart. Do you suppose one was my great-great-grandmother? I don't know her maiden name."

"You have relatives here, sweet pea?" Daisy patted the girl on the shoulder. "I had no idea." She seemed to realize that the rest of the group didn't really know the girl. "Mackenzie Floyd is a new and excellent addition to our team at the coffee shop," she told them.

"I can vouch for that," Maggie said, smiling.

"We're glad to have you, Mackenzie," Ruth said. "It's always nice to welcome someone with a connection to town."

Ina spoke. "Sarah Jane Mackenzie. Maybe your mother named you after her."

"You could be right. I don't really know why she named me Mackenzie, although there were a few Mackenzies in my high school." She went to her coat and pulled out an envelope.

"I brought a picture of my great-great-grandparents for you all to look at." She passed it around. "Mom is the one who told me they came from Somerset Harbor even though they were my dad's side of the family."

Maggie studied the photograph, a sepia-toned formal portrait of a pretty young woman seated in a chair. She wore a white Victorian wedding dress and a flower-topped veil. Her delicate fingers clasped a small bouquet, and a handsome bearded man dressed in a black suit stood behind her, his hand protectively on her shoulder. On the back was written, *Sarah and John Floyd, 189—*. The last digit was smudged.

"I wonder which Sarah might be Mackenzie's ancestor," Liz said. "Or whether Mackenzie's Sarah was even involved with this quilt."

"Well, it won't be Sarah Monroe," Ina said dolefully. "We know how that story ended."

"True," June said, "but there are two others. Sarah must have been a popular name back then."

"It still is," Maggie pointed out.

"Does your mother have any other information about Mr. and Mrs. Floyd?" Ruth asked, adjusting her glasses as she peered at the photograph, front and back.

Mackenzie shook her head, a look of sadness flitting over her features. "She, uh, passed away more than a year ago. She died from cancer." She looked down and cleared her throat.

"You poor thing! I'm so sorry to hear that," Daisy said. The others joined her in murmuring condolences.

The young woman appeared to shake off her sorrow and gave them a small smile. "Anyway, that's why I'm here. I don't have any relatives left, and I thought, why not find out more about Sarah and John? It gave me something to do." She looked at Maggie and then at Ina. "You know, I thought maybe I'd travel and find out about my ancestors for a while. This seemed like a good place to start."

And a way to escape Cody Becker, Maggie thought, though that hadn't worked out very well for the poor girl so far.

"We're going to help you figure this out," Liz said warmly. "I'll look through the church records for their marriage. My husband is the pastor at Old Faith Chapel."

"You can also come to the *Herald* and look for their engagement or wedding announcement," Adrian offered. "We have old editions stored in our archives."

"And they're hard copies," Ruth said proudly. "Not microfilm. You can also feel free to check out the historical society archives."

"This all sounds great." Mackenzie's grin was wide and genuine. "I really appreciate the help. It's going to be a fun project."

"And we can help Maggie learn more about the women who stitched the blocks," Fran suggested. "Maybe we can do a special exhibit and display information about each woman beside her square."

"It sounds like we're going to have our hands full between working on these special projects and raising money for the lighthouse," Ruth noted.

"I like being busy," Ina said in her spunky way. "It's the best way I know to fight cabin fever."

Her observation triggered commentary about the horrendous weather, and the meeting dissolved into a social gathering. Maggie moved between small groups, enjoying the sense of community she felt. How readily she had become part of this warm, close-knit group of women. She also enjoyed living in the same town as her ancestors, so she thoroughly understood Mackenzie's desire to learn more about her roots.

The meeting adjourned around nine, and Maggie ended up walking out with Mackenzie. "Did you enjoy tonight?" Maggie asked as she zipped up her coat in the hallway. The others filtered by, calling out good night as they exited.

"Oh yes," Mackenzie said. "History was my favorite subject in school, and it's even more fun when the research is about your own family."

"A woman after my own heart," Maggie said. "I moved here recently myself and I'm learning all kinds of things about my ancestors, the Sedgwicks. History and antiques have always been passions of mine and now I get to live and breathe them every day."

Mackenzie's eyes widened. "Do you live at Sedgwick Manor? I've seen it. It's beautiful!"

"Yes, I do. Come by anytime and I'll give you a tour. I'm usually either there or at Carriage House Antiques next to it. Or," she admitted with a grin, "at The Busy Bean."

"It seems like everyone in town goes there. I love that," Mackenzie said enthusiastically.

They stood on the granite steps, their breath visible in the frigid air. The thick clouds hadn't yet started dropping their load of snow, but they seemed threatening.

"I'm parked that way," Maggie said, pointing to her car. "How are you getting home?"

"Walking. It's not far. We live in an apartment over The Golden Chopsticks." The Chinese restaurant was only a couple of blocks away.

This corner of the street was quiet, lit by only a few streetlights and had very little traffic passing now that the meeting had dispersed. Maggie felt a shiver of unease. Somerset Harbor was a small town and usually safe, but after today's events, she felt concerned for the young woman's safety.

Across the street, in front of the elementary school, the streetlight was out, casting the area into deep shadow. In addition, a row of tall, thick evergreens made the area even darker. Was someone standing over there? Maggie strained her eyes, staring into the shadows and trying to discern if she really did see a person. Or was it just a figment of her imagination?

The figure moved. Yes, someone was over there, watching them. By the height, she guessed it was a man. Maggie made a fast decision. "Come on, Mackenzie. I'm taking you home."

Mackenzie shook her head. "Really, Maggie, I'm fine. It's just a couple of blocks."

Maggie checked to see if the man across the street was still there. He was, and it seemed like he was facing them. "Humor me, okay? I have a daughter about your age, and sometimes my motherly instincts go on high alert."

"Your motherly instincts?" Mackenzie giggled. "I guess I can't fight that."

As the duo trudged through the snow to the car, Maggie had the sense Mackenzie enjoyed feeling cared about. No wonder, since her mother had only recently died. And apparently her father wasn't in the picture either; she hadn't heard the young woman mention him at all. She felt a pang of sympathy for the waitress's loss. Emily certainly wasn't over the loss of her father; she would never wish the loss of both parents on someone so young. Maybe she should mobilize Daisy and the others to give Mackenzie extra doses of nurturing and care, especially until they knew Cody Becker had left town. They'd have to do it subtly, so as not to scare Mackenzie off.

Maggie unlocked the car and peeped across the street. Now she clearly saw that the figure was a man, and he was striding briskly away. Had he given up, or had he been innocent all along, just a local resident getting some air?

The chill racing down Maggie's spine as she climbed into the car and locked the doors convinced her that the man's intentions were anything but innocent.

Mackenzie had a stalker.

6

Insistent purring woke Maggie early the next morning. She opened her eyes and found herself nose to nose with Snickers.

"And good morning to you too." After stroking his head and chin, she scooted to a seated position. "I take it you're hungry."

In answer, he meowed and jumped down from the bed, then darted out of the bedroom toward the kitchen. Moving more slowly, Maggie fished around for her slippers and tied on a robe.

Like the rest of the mansion, this room was huge and furnished beautifully, this one in country French decor. Every morning, Maggie felt a rush of pleasure at waking up in such a pretty setting. It was more of a suite, really, with a bathroom the size of a small apartment. The windows also faced the ocean, and first thing every day, she opened the curtains to enjoy the landscape of sea and sky.

Today, whitecaps danced in a brisk onshore wind as shafts of sunlight breached the clouds, making the water glitter. With any luck, the snow would hold off.

She knew Snickers was waiting in the kitchen for her, but on the way, she made a detour to the front door to get the paper. *The Somerset Harbor Herald* was published weekly, and she happily paid the extra fee to have it delivered.

"Historical society plans to take over lighthouse," she read aloud as she entered the kitchen. She was impressed. Somehow Adrian had written the story and gotten it into this edition since last night's meeting. She set it on the table in the breakfast nook so that she could read it as she drank her coffee. Snickers rubbed against her legs and ran ahead of her to the cabinet where his food was stored. "I know, I know." She stroked his head and filled up his bowl. He attacked the dish as if he were starving.

Immediate crisis handled, she made coffee and plopped two pieces of bread into the toaster. Then she rummaged in the pantry for Ruth's homemade strawberry preserves. The small jar glowed scarlet, a sweet reminder of summer's bounty. She gazed out at the bleak winter landscape with a sigh. Spring couldn't come quickly enough.

Seated at the table, Maggie read over the article, which was supportive and encouraged those who wanted to help to contact the society. Below the fold was another article by Adrian, this one about the quilt blocks: "Antique Quilt Block Sheds Light on Mysterious Life of Vanished Heiress."

That is a bit of a stretch, she thought and chuckled. All they had learned from the blocks was that Sarah Monroe had contributed to the friendship quilt.

But why had the quilt blocks been made and never assembled? That was a mystery. Another was the lack of a block made by Julia Sedgwick.

Using Sarah Monroe's story, Adrian had tied the two articles together, conveying the importance of the lighthouse to the town's history. He'd also mentioned their quest to find out about Mackenzie's great-great-grandparents and listed all the names on the backs of the quilt blocks. Anyone who knew anything about the blocks' makers was encouraged to contact Ruth. *Very nicely done.* She popped the last bite of her toast into her mouth and chewed slowly, thinking about the articles. Setting the paper aside, she sipped the last of her coffee then stood. Time to shower, dress, and get to the shop. She and June had planned to talk about buying inventory.

About an hour later, when she entered the antiques shop, the first sight that greeted Maggie was James Bennett. He was hunkered down to examine a carved marble-top table. A flush of embarrassment swept over her, and she hesitated, remembering her impulsive answer to his invitation the night before.

He saw her, and a pale pink crept across his cheekbones. *He must feel the same discomfort,* she thought. For some reason, that made her feel better.

"Good morning," she said as she kicked off her boots. Then she unwound the scarf from around her neck. "How are you today?"

With a slight groan, he propped his hands on his knees and stood. "I'm fine. How about you?"

She forced a smile, determined not to be the more awkward one. "Great. What are you up to?" *Great question, Maggie. What does it look like he's up to?*

He ran his hand along the green marble. "I'm looking this over so I can figure out what needs to be done."

Maggie joined him. "Lovely piece." She bent to look at the ornate legs. "The work they used to do. It amazes me." She traced some of the carving with her fingers.

"All done by hand, that's for sure." James bent to show her a couple of spots where the veneer had chipped away, leaving bare spots of wood. "To restore it properly will mean matching the stain and finish exactly. I don't want to strip it since the rest of it is in good shape."

Maggie was impressed. "It looks like exacting work."

"It is." James took a deep breath and looked her in the eye. But before he could say anything, June bustled out of the back room.

"Good morning, Maggie. Interesting meeting last night, wasn't it?" She went to the counter and pulled the newspaper out of her bag. "Have you seen this yet?"

What had James been about to say? Did he regret asking her on the date? She didn't regret agreeing to go, did she?

Maggie forced herself to focus and respond to June with some intelligence. "Adrian did a nice job. I like the way he connected the two stories."

"Me too."

Maggie strolled over to the counter to stand near June. "It's fun to think something from the manor has a connection to one of the town's biggest mysteries."

James pulled a notebook out of his pocket and made notations. "Maybe you'll be able to find out what really happened to Sarah Monroe."

The idea made Maggie's pulse jump. She loved putting together pieces from the past to learn more about the people and stories behind antiques. Her aunt had felt the same way; she'd treasured the stories as much as the objects.

June looked amused. "Yes, Maggie. Solve the mystery. We'd get tons of PR for the lighthouse. Maybe even television exposure."

Maggie held up a hand. "Hold on. It was over a hundred years ago. Who knows what we'll be able to find out?"

June winked. "You're Evelyn's niece. And you've already solved a few mysteries since coming to our little town. I have faith in you."

"No pressure." Maggie rolled her eyes.

James tucked his notebook away. "Speaking of the lighthouse, you two are the first to know: We're calling a special meeting of the aldermen tonight."

"You mean the town will support us taking charge of it?" Maggie knew that towns could sometimes access grants and other funds.

"Perhaps. We'll need to vote. But I'll support it, of course. That lighthouse is a treasure." James headed for the coat rack. "I need to get going. See you two later." He pulled on his coat and wound his scarf around his neck, then left with a final wave and a tinkle of the bell on the door.

After they heard the engine of his Mercedes starting up, June said, "What was all that about?"

Maggie fiddled with a display of Victorian cranberry glass, lifting the stopper from a cruet and reinserting it. "What was all what about?"

June was almost smirking. "You could cut the tension in here with a knife." As Maggie remained silent, she added, "Of course, it's none of my business."

Maggie looked at June thoughtfully. She really needed to confide in someone, and June was probably the best person around. She was kind, discreet, and a good friend. "James asked me on a date."

June whooped. "That's great. I've been hoping you two would get together."

"On Valentine's Day."

The other woman's face fell. "Oh, I get it. That seems a bit premature, doesn't it?"

Maggie leaned back against the counter and folded her arms. "Yes, Valentine's Day has special meaning for couples. I don't know if I'm ready." Her eyes fell on the red-and-white vignette in the middle of the shop. "It's only been three years . . ."

"Say no more." June shook her head. "What was James thinking? You need to start out with coffee or lunch. Not *bam*, Valentine's Day. Where is he taking you? Did he say?"

"To the dinner at the Oceanview. I've heard it's nice. The Oceanview, that is. I haven't heard anything about the dinner." The grand old hotel had been built in the late 1800s and stood near the waterfront. Maggie had heard that it was beautifully decorated and lovingly restored.

"The dinner is spectacular. Kurt and I always go; it's an annual splurge. And it doesn't hurt that the hotel owner gives a portion of the proceeds to charity. We're doing a good deed while we dine on lobster in the middle of the winter." June grinned.

"That does sound nice." Maggie mulled over the situation. Part of her wanted to go, but another part was squawking, *No! It's too soon.* She sighed in frustration. "What do you think I should do?"

"I always say, go with your gut." June patted her midriff. "What's it telling you?"

"That's the problem. I'm getting mixed messages." Maggie sighed.

"Then I say talk to him. Tell him what you're thinking. You'll know what to do from his response." June patted Maggie's shoulder. "He's a good guy. It will all be fine."

Maggie's tension melted at June's suggestion. "Thanks." With an effort, she turned her thoughts firmly away from the topic of James. "You mentioned that we're getting low on inventory. What do you think we should look for?"

They spent the rest of the morning drawing up a list of furniture they needed so that they could meet requests from interior designers as well as from regular customers. Maggie had attended auctions, visited other dealers, checked the classifieds, and talked with people who wanted to sell their antiques to the shop. She knew it would be best for June to stay and keep the shop while Maggie went to look for new stock. She felt nervous and excited as June reiterated her confidence that Maggie was ready to take on this important step. As they prepared to stop for lunch, the phone rang. Maggie answered. "Good morning, Carriage House Antiques. How may I help you?"

There was silence for a moment, then a querulous voice asked, "Is this the antiques shop?"

"Yes, it is."

"This is Ruby Adams, out on Parker Road. I have some things I want to sell you."

"Great! Tell me about them." Maggie gestured at June to hand her a piece of scrap paper and a pen.

"Oh, I can't describe them," the elderly woman said. "You have to come out here. But they're worth it."

Despite Maggie's tactful efforts, she couldn't pry any information out of the woman. Finally she agreed to head right over, then hung up. She folded the paper in half and looked at June. "The good news is that I have an appointment to look at some pieces today."

"With whom?" June went to the small refrigerator and opened the door.

"A woman named Ruby Adams, out on Parker Road."

June snorted as she pulled out a container of homemade soup. "Sorry." She held up the container. "Want some? Kale and turkey meatball."

"Sounds delicious. My turn tomorrow." Maggie watched as June popped the soup into the microwave. "I'm guessing from your reaction that you know Ruby."

"I sure do. Sweet woman. But let me guess—she wouldn't tell you what she wants to sell." June found a couple of bowls and soupspoons in their small stash of dishes.

"That's right. How did you know?"

"She does the same thing to every dealer. I think she's lonely. We're probably her only visitors."

Maggie felt a pang of sympathy at the thought that Ruby had to sell her belongings to get someone to visit. "That's sad. No family?"

June shook her head. "Not that I know of. Her furniture is to die for, though. I drool every time I go out there. Of course, half the time she changes her mind and I come back empty-handed. So I really do think she's just lonely." She pulled the soup out of the microwave and served it into the bowls. "Grab the crackers, will you?"

Maggie found the sleeve of crackers in June's tote. "Maybe I should cancel."

"No, don't do that. You never know; Ruby might be in a selling mood today."

After lunch, Maggie bundled up and headed north out of town to visit Ruby. The route took her past the lighthouse, its tall, white tower majestic against a backdrop of sea and sky. Maggie could understand why the lovely building inspired artists and photographers. It made her think of the past, when sailing ships might have foundered on the rocky shore except for the saving grace of the lighthouse's beam. She hoped the historical society would be able to save it from development with the town's help.

Maggie told herself firmly that her excitement was for the aldermen's meeting itself, not the thought of seeing James there.

Fortunately Parker Road was marked by a sign, which was not a given in rural Maine. She followed a two-lane road into the rolling countryside. She was looking for a Cape Cod on the left, three miles down, according to June.

At two miles, she passed an interesting cluster of a farmhouse and outbuildings featuring a large red barn with a painted sign: Jed's Junk. The yard full of snow-covered objects spoke to the accuracy of the name. She should come back soon and check it out. June had described Evelyn's penchant for finding treasures in the most unlikely places.

The driveway to Ruby's house was short but not yet plowed, so Maggie parked along the road. The shingled house was set up on a small rise graced by an ancient maple tree and dormant lilac bushes on either side of the front door. A trickle of gray smoke rose from the chimney, a cozy sight on such a cold winter day.

As she started up the snowy drive, grateful she had worn boots, the front door flew open.

"Can you get my mail?" a tiny elderly woman called out. She

had curly gray hair and wore a cardigan over a floral housedress and a pair of fuzzy slippers.

Maggie noticed the mailbox by the road. "Of course." She doubled back, gathered the bundle of letters and newspapers, and trudged up the driveway, all under the woman's watchful eye.

"Don't come in this way," she called as Maggie stepped onto where she assumed the front path was located. "Come around to the kitchen." She pointed in the direction Maggie should go. Then she disappeared back inside.

As Maggie obeyed, she took in the house. By its size, small windows, and the center chimney, she guessed it was very old, perhaps from the 1700s.

"Seventeen ninety-eight," Ruby said as Maggie stepped into the kitchen, a cozy room with a chrome-trimmed cookstove and an ancient, rounded refrigerator. "People always ask, so I get that out of the way first."

Maggie looked around at the beamed ceiling and battered, wide-board floors. "I can see why. It's a lovely old place."

"Let me take your coat." Ruby reached for Maggie's parka and hung it on a peg by the door. "Flatlanders are always stopping by, trying to buy it." She snorted. "Like that handsome devil Tyler Monroe. He was here yesterday." She ushered Maggie toward the round oak table. "Have a seat. I've got the kettle on."

"Oh, you didn't need to go to that trouble." In spite of June's warning, Maggie had pictured being shown the merchandise, not sitting down for a social visit. *That'll teach me not to listen.* Ruby bustled around, pouring hot water into a teapot and pulling cups down from a cupboard.

"No trouble at all." Ruby carried the teapot to the table and then brought the cups and a pitcher of milk. The sugar bowl and spoons were already laid out. "There," she said, handing Maggie a cup of steaming tea. "Think we'll get snow again?"

Maggie resigned herself to sitting down for a visit. "I think we're supposed to, tonight." She thought about the blocked driveway. "Who plows your driveway?"

"Jed Parker." Ruby blew on her tea and took a sip. "He'll be along shortly, I'm sure. He's slow but steady."

"I drove by his place on the way. Does he sell good stuff?" Perhaps coming at the topic indirectly would ease Ruby in the right direction.

Ruby sniffed. "Mostly junk, as his sign says." She gave a sly grin. "Nothing like I've got." Her eye fell on the bundle of mail, and she began to look through it. Maggie sipped her tea, and Ruby glanced at the folded newspaper. "Anything good in there this week?"

"Actually, yes. At least I think so. The historical society is going to take over the lighthouse, if we can raise funds to restore and maintain it. Otherwise, they'll auction it."

"Oh my, that is news!" Ruby gasped. "Do you mind?" She adjusted her glasses, then scanned the article.

Regarding Maggie over the glasses, she said, "I hope you'll be able to save the lighthouse. Be a shame if one of those flatlanders got his mitts on it."

"A lot of people feel that way. There's a special town meeting tonight if you want to come."

"I don't go out at night since I stopped driving, but thank you." She indicated the feature on the quilt blocks. "What's this?" She began reading the article.

Maggie listened patiently.

Ruby slapped her hand on the table, startling Maggie. "Well, I can solve one mystery for you." She paused. "Sarah Jane Mackenzie was my great-aunt."

7

Maggie felt a thrill of excitement at Ruby's announcement. Had she found Mackenzie's great-great-grandmother already? "What can you tell me about her?"

Ruby pursed her lips, smoothing the newspaper with her hand. "Not a whole lot. My great-grandparents were among the rare few back then who supported women getting educated. Sarah Jane went to Radcliffe College in Cambridge, Massachusetts, and her brother, my grandfather, never saw her again. That's what my father said when I asked if he had any close relatives. Sarah Jane and my grandfather, Joseph Daniel, were the only two offspring in that branch of the Mackenzies."

Mackenzie was from Boston. "Did Sarah Jane get married?"

"I don't know. I suppose I could look through our old family papers and see what I can find."

"I would appreciate that, and it would be wonderful if you found a photograph. Last night at the historical society meeting, a young woman who is new to town, Mackenzie Floyd, showed us a picture of her great-great-grandparents. All she knows is that her great-great-grandmother came from Somerset Harbor and was named Sarah."

"Mackenzie, huh? People give their children the oddest names nowadays." Ruby put one hand to her cheek, her eyes widening. "Oh my. Maybe her mother gave her our family name and we're related."

"That's what I'm thinking. Of course, let's not be hasty. It could be a coincidence." Maggie prayed it wasn't. Mackenzie needed family and so did this sweet lady. "Oh, another thing.

We want to do an exhibit about the women who stitched the quilt blocks. We can include whatever you learn about your great-aunt."

"Sure! I'll pass along everything I find." Ruby pointed at the ceiling. "Somewhere up there is a box of old papers." She sighed heavily. "Of course I don't go up there much. My knees don't like those steep stairs . . ."

Maggie took the hint. "Do you want me to go look for them?" Inwardly she quailed. If Ruby's storage space was anything like the storage room or attic at the manor, she could be up there for hours.

Ruby flapped a dismissive hand. "No hurry. Have some more tea." She refilled their cups from the pot. "I'd like to see those blocks," she said wistfully, "especially the one Sarah Jane made."

Maggie had the blocks in the car since she was planning to drop them off at Fran's store on the way home. Fran wanted to examine them to see if they needed repair or restoration. "I happen to have them with me. Do you want me to go out to the car and get them? After I fetch the papers from upstairs, of course."

"Why, that would be lovely," Ruby told her. "I'll try not to take too much of your time."

· · · · · · · · · · · · · · · · ·

In spite of Ruby's promise, it was nearly five when Maggie arrived back in Somerset Harbor, which gave her only a few minutes to drop off the quilt blocks before Fran closed for the day. Traffic on Shoreline Drive was busy this time of night, with people dashing in and out of the stores before they closed or heading into restaurants for something to eat.

The lot next to The Busy Bean was full, so she slowed and scanned the spots on the right. She was in luck. A man was coming out of Fran's store and heading for a blue BMW parked in front, keys in hand. She braked back far enough to let him out, hoping to take his space.

As he pressed the key fob, making the lights blink, he looked around casually and his eyes met hers. It was Tyler Monroe, the handsome young man who made a habit of ruining historic properties, according to Ina, and trying to take advantage of elderly women, according to Ruby.

Tyler started the car, pulled out, and zoomed off, his tires throwing up slush. As Maggie pulled into the spot, she had to wonder why he'd been visiting Fran. He didn't look like a quilter. Then she scolded herself for being judgmental. She hadn't even spoken to the man.

"Hi, Maggie," Fran said as she entered the store. "I've been expecting you all afternoon." Her brow creased in a frown. "Although I'm glad you weren't here five minutes ago."

Maggie set the shiny box on the counter. "Does Tyler Monroe have anything to do with that remark?"

Fran's cheeks reddened and she dropped her gaze. "Everything."

She didn't elaborate, so Maggie changed the subject. "I was visiting Ruby Adams out on Parker Road today and guess what? Her great-aunt made one of the blocks." They'd never gotten around to looking at the furniture Ruby had claimed she wanted to sell. By the time she'd brought down the box of papers and showed Ruby her great-aunt's block, Maggie had been out of time. She'd have to set up another appointment.

Fran snapped out of her reverie. "Really? That's great. Which one was she?"

"Sarah Jane Mackenzie." Maggie gestured at the chest. "I assume you want a few days to look these over, so I'll leave them here." She glimpsed the wall clock. "I'd better get home so I can grab something to eat before the meeting tonight."

"Oh, that's right. The lighthouse meeting is tonight." Fran ran a hand along the smooth top of the box, still seeming distracted.

"I'll take good care of these for you—don't worry."

"I'm not a bit worried." Maggie hitched her purse up on her shoulder. "I need to get going. I'm sure Snickers is going crazy waiting for his supper."

"I bet he is. Give him a pat for me." Fran picked up the box. "I'll put this in the workroom." As she began to walk away, she called, "Thanks for stopping by. See you tonight."

Halfway to the door, Maggie stopped and turned around. "Do you think Tyler Monroe is related to Sarah Monroe?"

Fran paused in the doorway to the back room. "He might be. I don't know." She shrugged then added, "He said he was interested in the blocks." She bit her lip and ducked out of sight.

As Maggie pushed through the front door, the overhead bell jingling, she wondered what Tyler Monroe had done or said to fluster the normally serene Fran.

After a quick dinner of reheated chicken stew and biscuits, Maggie bundled up once more and drove into town for the aldermen's meeting. The three-story, brick town hall building was a few blocks up the hill from the harbor. Usually parking wasn't a problem, but tonight all the spaces near the municipal building were taken, and streams of people made their way along the sidewalks toward the entrance stairs. Apparently the people of Somerset Harbor were eager to make their opinions known on the matter of the lighthouse.

Maggie finally found a space in the corner of the school parking lot. Bracing herself for a cold trek in the dark, she locked the car and hurried toward the town hall. With a shiver, she remembered the man she had seen lurking in the shadows after the historical society meeting. Why hadn't she called June and gotten a ride? or picked up Ina?

The asphalt was fairly clear, but occasional patches of ice remained, and she had to be careful where she put her feet. Once she got to the sidewalk, she dashed from streetlight to streetlight, not wanting to linger in the dark between the pale yellow pools of light. Tall pines sighed and swayed in a sudden icy wind. Wincing, she tucked her chin deeper into her scarf.

Up ahead, the bright lights of the town hall beckoned like an oasis. *Not much farther now,* she told herself, wishing she weren't running late. The building steps were empty now, the double oak doors shut against the cold night.

Footsteps clattered behind her, the thump of heavy boots on tar. Another tardy meeting attendee . . . or was it? Her stomach lurched, and she broke into a jog.

The footsteps behind her sped up too. She braced herself. As the person drew closer, she peeked over her shoulder, hoping to see another innocent latecomer. As their eyes met, she gasped. It was Cody Becker, Mackenzie's former boyfriend. Tonight he wore a wool cap pulled low over his brow but she recognized his belligerent scowl.

He slowed to a walk. "Hey, I know you. Can you tell me where I can find Mackenzie Floyd?"

She finally reached the town hall and began to clamber up the wide granite steps, hoping to put distance between herself and the unruly young man. "No I can't. Even if I could, I wouldn't. I can't believe you have the nerve to ask."

"Ah, what do you know? I just want to talk to her." His voice was petulant and wheedling.

"Sorry. Can't help you." Resolutely ignoring him, Maggie puffed her way up the rest of the flight and entered the warm, lofty, safe building with a sigh of gratitude. She was thankful that Cody hadn't follow her.

When she opened the double doors to the meeting hall, she saw it was jammed with people; most of the folding seats were full, and people stood along the back wall. The six aldermen sat on a low dais at the front of the room facing the audience. James was speaking. "Hey, folks. I know it's a cold night and most of you would rather be home by the fire, so let's get started."

Everyone settled down to listen. Maggie slipped inside, nodding at Ina's nephew, police officer Robert Linton, who stood next to the door. He was on duty, judging by his uniform. Robert winked at her and pointed to a seat about halfway down the aisle. Feeling terribly conspicuous, Maggie tiptoed across the shiny hardwood floor to the vacant seat. She nodded a greeting at the person next to her—a heavyset woman she didn't know—and pulled off her coat as quietly as possible.

At James's request, Ruth Harper moved to the front of the room and addressed the group regarding the government's offer to give the lighthouse to the historical society.

As she listened, Maggie perused the room, wondering if Mackenzie was there. If so, Maggie would have to warn her that Cody Becker might be lurking outside after the meeting. In any case, maybe she could persuade Mackenzie to talk to Robert about her ex-boyfriend's aggressive behavior.

She didn't see Mackenzie, but she did see that the rest of the historical society was out in full force tonight. Daisy even had her husband, Harry, with her, and June her husband, Kurt. Fran was seated right across the aisle, and when Maggie caught her eye, she gave her a wave, noticing that her friend still seemed out of sorts. She also noticed reporter Adrian Diaz in the front row, busily taking notes and snapping an occasional picture.

After Ruth finished, James gave the floor to other residents who wanted to speak. As they stood, they uniformly discussed the value of the lighthouse to the town, both as a tourist draw and as a cherished part of Somerset Harbor's history.

One dignified old gentleman in a plaid flannel shirt and work pants shared a story from his World War II–era boyhood.

"I'll never forget the day they finally gave the order to put the lighthouse back in service. Everyone in town gathered on the cliffs or out on boats in the bay to wait for the Coast Guard to switch on the light." He paused for a moment, obviously moved, and Maggie felt her own eyes welling in response. She blinked rapidly, hoping no one would notice.

The man patted his chest with his fist. "I was so proud when that big beam swept across the water for the first time in years. It was good to know the Somerset light was back in business, saving sailors and ships from hitting them nasty rocks. Thank you." He lurched down into his seat to uproarious applause. By the cleared throats and appearance of tissues, Maggie guessed his story had affected many others in the audience.

After a respectful moment or two, James asked, "Would anyone else like to speak?" At that moment, the swinging double doors at the back of the room banged open. Tyler Monroe stood in the doorway, casually elegant in an expensive overcoat, cashmere scarf, and fine leather gloves. He appeared unperturbed by the crowd of eyes suddenly trained on him. "I'd like to say something," he said, his deep voice carrying easily as he walked toward the back row of seats.

James waited for him to walk forward, close enough for the audience to hear him clearly. "Go ahead, Mr. Monroe," he then said with a nod.

"I intend to buy the lighthouse."

The audience reacted to this bold statement with gasps and cries of protest. Tyler waited until everyone quieted again. "I know my proposal might not be popular." Hisses and whispers met that statement. "But I really doubt this little society will be able to raise the funds to restore that old hulk."

The old man stood and shook his finger at Tyler. "Don't underestimate us, young man. That's *our* lighthouse."

Tyler's smile skated on the edge of a smirk. "With all due respect, it's going to take someone like me to save it." He nodded regally at the rapt and outraged crowd. "Think about it." With that, he turned and walked out of the door.

A maelstrom of voices broke out and James had to use his gavel to restore order. Once everyone fell silent, he calmly thanked everyone for coming to the meeting and especially for offering their thoughts and suggestions. Then he closed with, "We have our work cut out for us regarding the lighthouse. For those who would like to help, please see Ruth Harper or a member of the historical society after the meeting." He turned to the other aldermen. "Who wants to make a motion to adjourn?"

After the official meeting was adjourned, people milled about during a social time, drinking coffee and munching on snacks. Many townsfolks approached June or a member of the historical society to offer their help. When the initial rush calmed down, Maggie bought a homemade raspberry-filled cookie sold by volunteers from the fire department. She was filling a paper cup with decaf when she felt a tug at her sleeve. She turned to see Ina dressed in wool camo pants and a cream fisherman's-knit sweater.

"What did you think of that meeting?" Ina asked. "I can see we've got a fight on our hands." In contrast to the downcast demeanor of some of the other town residents, Ina appeared energized by the battle.

Maggie moved away from the table and took a bite of the cookie. It melted in her mouth, leaving behind a jolt of tart fruit. When she could speak, she said, "I'm not willing to give up that easily. I think we should give it our best shot."

"Yes!" Ina pumped a fist. "I knew you'd see it that way. We're kindred spirits."

Maggie smiled. She certainly admired the woman's determination and lack of fear when confronting problems, even when the "problem" was an large, angry young man.

Ina glanced around then leaned forward and whispered conspiratorially, "You know what we should do first?"

Maggie took a sip of coffee. "What's that?"

"We need to go out to the lighthouse and take a look." Ina shrugged. "We don't even know the size of the nut we need to crack yet."

"I agree," Maggie said, smiling because she had suggested that very thing at the historical meeting. "I'd love to look at the lighthouse. But we can only see the outside, right?"

"No ma'am." Ina patted one of her pants pockets. "I've got a key."

"It's a date! When should I pick you up?"

"Ten o'clock tomorrow morning." Ina grabbed Maggie's arm and leaned close. "Think you could give me a ride home?" Ina looked over her shoulder and rolled her eyes at the remaining stragglers behind her. "I'm ready to blow this joint."

Maggie was grateful to have Ina's feisty companionship on the walk out to the dark and lonely parking lot. After dropping Ina off at her house, Maggie headed for the manor with a sense of relief. It had been a long, tiring day, and it felt like she had been on the go every minute. Two evening meetings in a row were also exhausting.

As she pulled into the driveway, her mind eased in anticipation of a hot shower and bed. Snickers would need a good, long cuddle session too. She'd neglected him horribly all day, a state of affairs she knew he found unacceptable.

Since she was going out in the morning, she pulled the car around the circular drive to the front door instead of parking in the garage. There was no snow in the forecast tonight. She readied her house keys as she hurried toward the house, eager to get inside.

As she pulled open the storm door, a piece of paper that had been tucked in the jamb fell to the porch floor. Assuming it was a flyer advertising home repairs or a restaurant menu, she picked it up and gave it a rudimentary glance.

What she read made her blood run cold.

Mind your own business—or else.

8

Maggie stared at the nasty note written in crude handwriting, her hand beginning to tremble. Who would have left such a thing? And why? Her impulse was to crumple it and toss it into the snowbank, but she knew better than that. She needed to call the police.

Unable to tear her eyes away from the note, she somehow unlocked the door and pushed her way inside. Then she dropped her handbag on the floor, placed the note on the side table, and found her phone.

Snickers ran into the foyer, meowing. Absently, she bent to pet him while waiting for the call to connect.

"Evening, Maggie. What can I do for you?"

"Robert, I'm so glad you picked up. I've got kind of a . . . situation here, but I didn't think it warranted a call to 911." She described the threatening note.

"Why don't I come over now? I can swing by on my way home."

He must still be at the town hall. Relief coursed through Maggie at the realization she wouldn't have to wait long. "If it's not too much trouble, that would be great."

After she hung up, she circled the house, checking the windows and doors to make sure everything was locked up tight. Snickers followed her the entire way, staring up at her as if wondering what his human was up to now.

"I know, Snickers. I'm being silly. No one came inside as far as I can tell." Maggie led the way into the kitchen, where she put on the kettle for a soothing cup of herbal tea. Otherwise she would surely be in for a restless night. She probably still would anyway. She stared at the note. How could such an innocent object hold such venom? It was like having a snake curled up on her vestibule table.

She refilled Snicker's food dish, brewed her tea, and sat down in the breakfast nook.

A rapping on the side-door announced Robert, and she jumped up to let him in. "Thanks for coming over. I'm sure you're eager to get home after a long day."

"Not a problem." Hands on hips, the officer took a gander around, a concerned expression on his boyish face. About Maggie's age, Robert had close-cropped dark hair and a good crop of freckles across his cheeks. "Any signs that someone got inside?"

Maggie shook her head. "No, thank goodness. The note was tucked in the front door."

"Show me." He followed Maggie back into the foyer. She showed him where she'd found the note, and then he read it, being careful not to touch it.

"I was wearing gloves, so hopefully you'll be able to get some fingerprints off it," she said.

Robert shook his head. "I doubt it. But we'll try of course." He slid the note into an evidence envelope, which he sealed, signed, and dated. "Any thoughts on who might have left it?"

"Not really." Then Maggie remembered Cody Becker's anger toward her. "There is one person who might not be particularly happy with me." She went on to explain her encounters with Cody Becker. While she spoke, Robert took notes.

Robert was obviously amused by Maggie's description of his elderly aunt reprimanding the young man for shaking a woman. "She certainly rushes in where angels fear to tread," he said fondly. On a more serious note, he asked, "Do you think this Cody Becker knows where you live?"

"I have no idea. But I'm sure most people do, so if he asked around, he could have found out." Somerset Harbor was a small town, something that was both comforting and alarming, depending on whether you needed help or were trying to keep a secret.

"So there's nothing else going on that would upset anyone?" Robert frowned.

Maggie wracked her brain. "No," she finally said, "not a thing that I can think of. I found some old quilt blocks, and I'm going to help the historical society find money for the lighthouse, but I don't see how either of those things could upset someone."

Robert raised his brows. "Those both seem fairly harmless. Before I go, I'll go around outside and check the doors and windows." He adjusted his hat more firmly on his head. "Call me immediately if anything else strange happens."

. . . .

To Maggie's surprise, she actually slept all night without tossing and turning. She didn't know whether to credit Robert's comforting presence or the herbal tea. Either way, the unpleasant note felt like a fading nightmare, and she resolutely prevented it from creeping into her mind again.

The brilliant sunshine that greeted her when she pulled open the bedroom curtains helped brighten her mood even more. She smiled when the warm sunlight beamed through the window and touched her face.

"It's going to be a good day, Snickers," she said. "I can feel it." He meowed and followed at her heels as she bustled to the kitchen. There she gave him his breakfast and whipped up a cheese-and-mushroom omelet with wheat toast for herself.

As she crunched the last bite of her toast, her cell phone rang. Ina Linton's number flashed on the screen.

"Good morning, Ina. Are we still on for this morning?" Now that the outing was upon her, she realized how much she wanted to explore the lighthouse.

Ina snorted. "Of course. We're in luck—it's a nice day. But even if it wasn't, we've got to get over there and check out the old girl. I'm bringing a notepad so we can take notes on what needs to be done. Might save James some time."

"I'll bring my digital camera and take some pictures," Maggie offered. "Then James will have pictures to go with the notes." She wondered how long it would be before she could think of him without feeling ashamed of her hasty acceptance of his invitation to the Valentine's dinner.

"Good idea. A picture is worth a thousand words, right? So when will I see you? Ten still?"

"I'll be right over after I shower and dress."

"You're a late riser, aren't you?" Ina said bluntly. "I've been up since five." She snorted again. "No matter. I'll be ready when you get here."

"Great, I'll see you—"

Ina interrupted. "Oh, I called to tell you to dress warm. It's going to be pretty cold in that building. They keep the heat at the minimum to save money; it's usually on just enough to keep the pipes from freezing."

"Thanks for the advice. I'll dig out my long johns."

When Maggie pulled into Ina's driveway, she saw the front curtain twitch. When Ina emerged through the kitchen door, Maggie had to stifle a laugh at her getup. Ina wore a bulky Army winter parka, snow pants with gaiters clasped around her calves, and a wool ski mask that covered all of her face except her eyes.

"I see you're dressed for the cold," Maggie commented as Ina slid into the passenger seat.

Ina tugged the mask off her head, releasing her wispy, white hair. "Do you like my balaclava? All the winter climbers wear them. Protects your skin from frostbite *and* premature aging." She squinted at Maggie. "You might want to consider getting one."

"Gee, thanks." Maggie chuckled and put the car into reverse. "All set?"

"Let me get buckled." Ina fastened her seat belt. "I just meant that you have lovely skin, and it would be a shame if it got chapped. A mask will help."

"I'll keep that in mind." Maggie backed down the driveway and headed toward the lighthouse.

A group of children were building a snowman in a neighbor's yard. As they passed, Ina pulled the mask back over her face. "Honk the horn," she said.

Maggie complied, wondering what on earth Ina was up to now. Ina opened the window, and as the air rushed in with a roar, shook her fist at the kids, who turned to stare at her. One little girl screamed and clutched at an older child. But the boys bellowed with laughter, leaning over and clutching their sides. "Good one, Miss Linton!" one called.

"You scared that little girl," Maggie scolded lightly.

Ina shut the window, cackling. "We have a game going on, me and the O'Brien kids. They try to scare me and I try to scare them. Nothing serious. They got me good last week with a mask taped to my window."

Would she be so youthful at Ina's age? Maggie hoped she'd have some of Ina's youthfulness.

The ride out of town was pleasant on such a clear day, the bright sunshine belying the bitter temperatures. The roads were clear of snow for a change, gray with salt and sand.

"There's Monroe Mansion," Ina said.

Maggie followed Ina's point and looked up a long driveway.

She gasped at the sight of the majestic structure. The mansion featured a mansard roof, a rectangular central tower, and bay windows sprinkled along the first floor. The paint job was pale gray with white trim; dark-gray shingles covered the roof.

"It's gorgeous," Maggie said. "Although that style seems to be used a lot in movies with haunted houses."

"It's haunted, all right. By the spirit of greed," Ina said darkly. "Tyler Monroe lives there now."

A short distance past the mansion, they turned onto the lighthouse access road, part of which was plowed to make room for several vehicles. A small, dented, blue sedan sat there, the only other car in the lot.

"Whose car could that be?" Ina asked, staring at it as they pulled in and stopped a short distance away. "I don't recognize it."

"It has Massachusetts plates," Maggie said. Now that they were at the lighthouse, she dreaded getting out of the warm car. A whipping wind blew loose snow across the open bluff where the lighthouse stood. She pulled her hat down farther over her ears and popped on sunglasses against the glare. "Ready?"

"I am if you are." Ina adjusted the mask and lifted the hood on her jacket over her head as well. She flung open the car door. "'Once more unto the breach.'"

Maggie recognized the quote from Shakespeare's *Henry V*. "'Lay on, MacDuff,'" she offered in return, borrowing from *Macbeth*. She opened her own door and shuddered as the cold air assaulted her.

"Good job!" Ina shouted over the howling wind. "You got that right. Most people say 'lead on,' if they know the quote at all." She bent her head and trudged toward a snowbank at the edge of the parking area. Previous walkers had cut a passage over it in one spot.

As she followed Ina, eyes watering, Maggie studied the

lighthouse. It stood calm and dignified against the heaving water beyond the cliff. An attached rectangular structure in the rear must have been where the keeper lived.

Tracks from a previous visitor led toward the building. The two women walked the same route, and about halfway there, someone came around the corner of the keeper's house. They drew closer until Maggie recognized Mackenzie, dressed in a thick parka and snow pants, carrying a knapsack. "Hi, Mackenzie," she called. "What are you doing out here?"

Mackenzie darted a look at Ina's mask, and a grin flashed across her pretty face. "Freezing. I should get one of those."

"You should," Ina said. "My face is nice and toasty right now."

Maggie wished she could say the same. Her cheeks, nose, and chin were rigid with cold.

"I bet." Mackenzie turned back to Maggie. "Actually I was doing some sketching. The wind's not too bad on the other side of that building. There's a sheltered spot. Are you two here to check out the lighthouse for the historical society?"

"Exactly." Ina patted her pocket. "I have a key to the inside. Want to come with us?"

Mackenzie fell into step with them. "I'd love to. I've always been fascinated by lighthouses."

"Me too," Maggie said. "I've always thought it would be so much fun to live in one."

Ina inserted the key in the old-fashioned lock on the keeper's house, and with a few grunts and kicks, she managed to open the door. They stepped into a vestibule where a row of hooks on one wall evoked images of oilskins and boots from days past. Beyond it was the main room made up of a combination kitchen and living room judging by the cookstove, oak kitchen table, and overstuffed sofa and armchair. A calendar dated 1976 still hung on the pale-green plaster wall.

Ina nodded at the calendar. "That's when they automated the light and the keeper moved away."

Despite the air of neglect and age, the place had a quaint charm. Maggie's fascination grew as she looked over the unique dwelling space.

Mackenzie seemed enchanted too, a broad grin on her face as she gazed around. She went to the shelf over the double porcelain sink and examined the white-and-green dishes. "It's like they just walked out and left everything behind."

"All these furnishings came with the place," Ina said. "The same family ran the lighthouse for several generations. One of my good friends grew up here. She still lives pretty close, in Portland."

"Was that family here during Sarah Monroe's day?" Maggie asked.

"I'll find out. I like the way you think. Maybe we can approach the mystery from a different direction."

"Are you trying to find out what happened to Sarah Monroe?" Mackenzie asked. She plopped down on the sofa, which released a huge cloud of dust. Surprised, she sprang back to her feet.

"Maybe," Maggie said. "An entry in my aunt's journal got me wondering if there was more to the story." She told her the cryptic message Evelyn had included in the journal.

"I wish I had an aunt who left me a mysterious journal with clues," Mackenzie said enviously.

Her wistful words reminded Maggie about meeting the lonely Ruby Adams. "I meant to tell you, Mackenzie. We may have found your Sarah already. Nothing definite, but it's a possibility."

Mackenzie clapped her gloved hands, her eyes gleaming with excitement. "That's amazing. Which one was it?"

"Well, I'm not sure, but it might have been Sarah Jane Mackenzie. Her great-niece lives in town. She's planning to do a little digging to see if she can find Sarah Jane's married name or anything that might tell us more about her."

Ina snapped her fingers. "Ruby Adams, right? I should have thought of her. Good work, Maggie."

"Can I meet her soon?" Mackenzie asked.

"I'll call her and ask," Maggie promised. The room's low temperature was beginning to penetrate her bones, so she asked Ina, "Is there more to see?"

"Certainly. Follow me and we'll do the building inventory." Ina put her hands on her hips and examined the room. "This room needs to be plastered and painted." She kicked at the peeling fake-brick linoleum. "I'll bet there's wood under this. We should pull it up and sand the floors."

"The windows look rotten too." Mackenzie pointed to spots on the sills and jambs where the wood was cracked and warped. It looked like water had leaked in and made the paint flake.

"Let's measure those," Ina said. She pulled a tape measure out of her jacket pocket and, with Mackenzie's help, calculated the dimensions of all the windows. "These will have to be resealed."

Maggie duly made notes, and then they trooped after Ina into the office. Here a rolltop desk sat under a window overlooking the ocean, the logbook open to the last page a keeper had made a notation. A brass telescope lay on the top shelf of the desk, and an assortment of barometers and other weather equipment hung nearby. Marine charts filled the left wall while on the right sat old logbooks stacked on a bookshelf. An assortment of snapshots and pictures had been pinned to the plaster above.

Mackenzie went right to the photographs. "Do you think you could be in one of these, Ina? I mean, since your friend grew up here?"

Ina and Maggie joined her. "I might be." She pointed to a faded Polaroid showing several young women and a teenage boy dressed in the fashion of the early 1960s and perched on the rocks out front. "There I am!" Ina said.

Back then, Ina had sported a blond pageboy hairstyle, but her mischievous grin certainly hadn't changed.

"Who are the rest of those people?" Mackenzie asked.

"My friend and her siblings." Ina pointed to each, giving their names.

Maggie's eye was caught by a much older, sepia-tone photograph. Like the one with Ina, it depicted a group of young women, though there were more of them in this one, and it was clearly much older. The image showed more than a dozen women in long dresses or skirts with shirtwaists. Their hair was piled on their heads, and they wore delicate hats.

A trickle of excitement ran down her spine. Could it be the group who had made the quilt blocks? She carefully pried up the thumbtack securing the photograph to the wall and turned the picture over. *Success!* A list of names followed the caption *Quilting Guild, 1898.* Sarah Monroe was there, as well as the other Sarahs, Maggie's great-grandmother, and the other names written on the blocks.

"Ina, take a look at this." Ina and Mackenzie gathered around her. "Which one is your grandmother?"

"Let me see." Ina squinted, holding the photograph close, then out at arm's length. "Yes, that's her, third from the right." Nellie had light hair and a grin that rivaled her granddaughter's in mischief.

"Darn. The names aren't in order." Maggie had hoped to match the names with the faces, thereby matching Mackenzie's ancestor to a name and also getting a glimpse of the mysterious heiress, Sarah Monroe.

"They're alphabetical," Mackenzie pointed out. She studied the photo closely, then dropped her pack from her shoulders. "Hold on a minute."

She pulled out the picture of her great-great-grandparents. After placing the two photographs side by side, the three of them positively identified one of the women in the photo as the future Sarah Floyd.

"This is awesome," Mackenzie said, her cheeks flushed with excitement. "Now I know for sure my great-great-grandmother came from here."

"And sewed one of the quilt blocks, I bet," Maggie added.

"I wish we could take this photo," Mackenzie said. "Or get a copy."

"We can ask the Coast Guard to make us a copy," Ina suggested. "They're pretty obliging."

"Good idea." Maggie pulled out her phone. "But meanwhile, I'm going to take a picture of this for reference." She placed the photograph on the desk and took pictures of the front and back.

"Can you email that to me?" Mackenzie asked.

"Of course." Maggie tucked the phone away. "What's next, Ina?"

Before the other woman could answer, the outside door opened with a squeak and closed with a thud, making them all jump.

"Are we expecting someone else?" Maggie asked Ina in a whisper.

"Not that I know of," Ina said. "I didn't tell anyone we were coming out here."

"Who's there?" Maggie called.

There was no answer except the sound of heavy footsteps thumping across the creaky floor.

Maggie tensed as the footsteps came closer. What if it was Cody Becker, come to accost Mackenzie again? She stared around for a weapon, should one be required, but there wasn't much available except the old brass telescope. Using such a nice antique that way would be a shame.

Tyler Monroe appeared in the doorway, his rubber-soled boots the only concession to the harsh winter conditions. Otherwise he wore a cashmere overcoat and leather gloves, without a hat to muss his sculpted blond hair—attire more suited to city streets than rural Maine. He nodded to each in turn, his eyes lingering on Mackenzie, who gave a little wave. "Hello, ladies."

"What are *you* doing here, Monroe?" Ina fairly spit his name. She stepped protectively between him and her friends, as if she weren't the smallest person in the room.

"Same as you, Ina—checking out the lighthouse." Tyler looked at Mackenzie as he removed his gloves. "We met at the coffee shop," he said, then he thrust his hand toward Maggie. "I don't think we've officially been introduced."

She shook his hand. "I'm Maggie Watson. I own Carriage House Antiques on Shoreline Drive. Perhaps you've seen it." As always, the mention of her business gave her a little thrill.

"Nice to meet you." Tyler's hand was warm and a little clammy. Was he nervous? Standing closer to him, she noticed how good-looking he was, with regular features and a square jaw. But there was a hard, glittering light in his blue eyes that marred his looks. Then he blinked and it was gone, replaced by a congenial smile.

"I may have some antiques for you to buy. I'm cleaning out the house, making room for some furniture that's more to my taste."

Ina bristled at this remark. "The Monroe Mansion is exquisitely furnished. It's a shame to break up the family's belongings."

Tyler's lip curled. "If you like that kind of thing. I prefer modern styles."

"That's what keeps me in business," Maggie said lightly, hoping to diffuse the tension. "People buying new things and cleaning out their houses." She sympathized with Ina and shared her preferences in furnishings, but no good would come from antagonizing Tyler Monroe.

"Are you related to Sarah Monroe?" Mackenzie asked Tyler. "I heard about her disappearance at the historical society meeting."

"Yes, I am. After she vanished, the house passed to a cousin. I'm descended from that branch."

"My relatives came from Somerset Harbor too," Mackenzie said eagerly. "The society is helping me track them down."

"How nice." Wandering over to the desk, Tyler peered out the window at the view, giving a low whistle. "Spectacular."

Ina shot a glare at his back. "I think we're done in here, so let's go up the tower," she said firmly to Maggie and Mackenzie.

"I can't wait to go up there," Mackenzie said. "I've always wanted to see inside a lighthouse tower."

To Ina's visible dismay, Tyler tagged along. "Me too."

To reach the tower, they ascended a flight of stairs to the second floor. Here, three bedrooms were located off the hall. They toured those briefly, and Maggie noted the repairs needed for the leaking ceilings and peeling wallpaper. Then, through a fourth door off the hall, they found a spiraling metal staircase that led up to the light.

"Onward and upward." Ina gestured for them to follow. "I hope none of you are afraid of heights." The ornate staircase wound along the inside of the exterior wall, providing a rather precipitous view down through the middle to the bottom.

"I'm not," Maggie said, although she was glad to note that the tower was free of spiders and cobwebs. As she trudged up the stairs, holding the rail as she went, she heard Mackenzie bubbling away to Tyler about her quest to find her family.

"All I know is her name was Sarah," she was saying. "And we've got three Sarahs to choose from."

"Really. Three?"

"Yes, if you count Sarah Monroe. But of course she never had kids, right?"

"Not as far as I know" was the terse reply.

Maggie got the feeling Tyler wouldn't welcome news of a newfound relative. That reminded her that she needed to call Ruby once they were done with the tour. Even if Ruby and Mackenzie weren't related, maybe they could become friends.

"Here we are," Ina said, opening the door at the top of the stairs. The round chamber was surrounded entirely by glass with an outside catwalk accessed by another door.

"Where's the light?" Mackenzie asked, looking around the room. Other than a short ladder leading upward to a hatch, the room was empty.

Ina pointed up. "Above our heads. One of the few remaining Fresnel lenses being used."

She went on to describe the historic lens that could beam light over long distances.

The outside railing was covered with ice and snow, so Maggie contented herself with circling the room inside to enjoy the 360-degree view. On such a clear day, she could see the inland hills, their snow-covered tops catching the sun. In the other direction, the jagged edge of the coastline stretched north and south while to the east, the ocean touched the horizon.

A tanker ship chugged slowly along, heading for port.

"Spectacular," she murmured, lost in the vista of sea and sky.

"Yes, isn't it?" Tyler appeared at her elbow. "You can see why I want to make this into a very special home."

Ina was at her other side. "The lighthouse would make a wonderful *museum*. Can't you imagine the hordes of happy visitors enjoying this view next summer?"

The two glared at each other, with Maggie caught in the middle.

"I have an idea," Mackenzie piped up, hands on her hips. "When I find my long-lost family, I'll buy it and let the public tour. And give the proceeds to the society." Judging by the cheeky grin on her face, she was joking, to Maggie's relief.

Apparently Tyler wasn't amused; he merely grunted. "Good luck to you, Ina. I hope the society can raise the money. But I doubt it." He whirled around, open coat and scarf swinging, and left, his footsteps clanging down the metal stairs.

"What a spoilsport," Mackenzie said, gazing after him.

"That's one word for it," Ina muttered. "Now, Maggie, I think this room could use new weatherproof windows . . ."

By the time they finished the inspection to Ina's satisfaction, Maggie was chilled to the bone. Mackenzie suggested heading to The Busy Bean for lunch, since she had to work anyway, and Maggie agreed completely. Ina didn't say so, but Maggie suspected she was looking forward to a hot lunch too as she climbed back into Maggie's car.

As soon as they stepped through The Busy Bean's door, the steamy, busy café made Maggie's spirits rise—and her fingers and toes begin to thaw.

Ina had decided to wear her mask inside, and they garnered more than their fair share of stares as they slid next to Maggie's favorite table overlooking the water. Mackenzie disappeared to clock in, assuring them that she'd eat when the café had a slow spell. Daisy bustled up with the coffeepot while they were taking off their coats. "Where y'all been? The North Pole?" Today Daisy's hair was piled up in a beehive, one of her favorite styles.

"We went to the lighthouse to inspect the premises," Ina said. "Preliminary to asking James to give us an estimate."

"How was it?" Daisy pulled creamers out of her apron pocket and set them on the table.

"It could be worse," Maggie said. "But of course we'll want the repairs to be historically appropriate, which might add cost."

Ina grunted. "Unlike the job that weasel Tyler Monroe will do. He'll rip everything out and put up some modern rubbish." She waved a finger at Daisy. "Would you believe he had the nerve to show up today and look around like he owned the place already?"

Daisy coughed. She and Ina tended to disagree on other matters, and Daisy was as passionate in her arguments as Ina. But here, they were in agreement. "Well, how do you like that? That man doesn't know how to use his head to keep the rain out of his neck!"

"Daisy, could I have a club sandwich and sweet-potato chips?" Maggie interrupted politely as Ina opened her mouth. If she didn't nip this in the bud, Daisy and Ina would just build off each other and they'd never get lunch.

Maggie's request apparently reminded Ina why they were there, and her appetite seemed to win out over her righteous indignation, at least for the moment. "I want hot soup, lots of it," Ina said. "I see you have beef barley."

"Good choices," Daisy said, switching back to hostess mode. "Your lunches will be right out." Then she leaned closer to Ina and murmured, "We'll finish our chat later. We need to settle that Tyler Monroe." Daisy hurried off to put in their orders.

"What are you doing this afternoon, Ina?" Maggie asked.

Ina yawned and stretched. "I'm going home to watch my shows and take a nap. I'm plumb tuckered out."

Maggie was too, but she couldn't picture herself taking a midday nap. "After I drop you off, I think I'll go over to the newspaper archives and see what I can find out about the Sarahs."

They ate heartily, and afterward, Maggie drove Ina home, then headed over to the *Herald*'s offices located across from the town hall on Monroe Avenue. *The Monroes must have been very prominent in town to have a street named after them,* she thought. It was a shame their descendant was more interested in personal profit than the town's welfare.

As she found a spot and parked, her cell phone rang. *Emily!* She grabbed it eagerly and answered.

"Hey, sweetie. What's up?"

"Not much." Emily gave a big yawn. "I've got another class this afternoon, but I'd rather take a nap."

"Me too, but I'm at the newspaper to do some research instead."

"Really? I can let you go if you're busy."

"No, it's okay. I haven't gone in yet. What's new?"

"Well." Emily gave another yawn. "I'm going to a Valentine's Day dance."

Maggie's heart skipped a beat. Was Emily moving on after all? That thought keenly reminded her of her situation with James. Was *she* moving on?

"With a date?" Maggie managed to keep her tone light. She had to be careful not to probe.

"Nope. I told Ian I'm not quite ready for that, and he understood. It'll be a group of us, boys and girls. You met some of them when we were there for Thanksgiving."

"That's right. Nice kids." Maggie hesitated. She wanted to tell her daughter about the date with James in case she did go and someone else mentioned it to Emily. She wanted her daughter to hear it from her. "Um, Emily? I might have plans for Valentine's Day too."

Emily's tone perked up. "Really? What's going on?"

"James Bennett asked me out to dinner, to a charity benefit at the Oceanview Hotel." She held her breath, waiting for Emily's reaction.

"I've heard the Oceanview has awesome food. Are you going?"

To Maggie's relief, her daughter appeared to be taking the date in stride, even excited about it. "I said yes, but to be honest, I'm having doubts." She paused. "We haven't even been on an official date, and Valentine's seems . . ."

"Too much too soon? Yeah, I can see that. But there's no reason not to go. Just tell him you're going for the food, not the romance. And to help a good cause, of course." Emily's voice had an air of playfulness.

Maggie laughed, more with relief than at her daughter's joke. "I'm not sure how that would go over, but thanks. I'll talk to him and let him know I want to move slowly." Then she added hastily, "If we're moving forward at all, that is. Jury's still out on that one."

"Don't worry, Mom. I know you won't be alone forever. I don't think Dad would like that, and neither would I." With that breezy remark and a promise to call again soon, Emily hung up.

Bemused, Maggie stared through the windshield at the bright blue sky. Who would have guessed her daughter of all people would encourage her to pursue a new relationship? Feeling suddenly carefree, she tucked the phone into her purse and opened the door. Time to do some research . . . and maybe solve a mystery or two.

The well-worn but serviceable newspaper office had had a few changes since Maggie had last stopped in. The vintage orange vinyl visitor chairs, racks of newspapers, and glass-topped wooden counter were the same, as was the pungent smell of printer's ink. But Thaddeus Jablonsky, the editor, wasn't working alone anymore. A heavy oak desk had been placed facing his, and Adrian sat there, typing away in tandem with Thad. Both men looked up from their computers when she entered, her footsteps on the mat triggering a buzzer. That was also new.

"Got some news for us, Ms. Maggie? Or maybe an ad for your business?" Thad's smile was hopeful.

"You know, that's not a bad idea, putting in an ad for the Carriage House," Maggie said. "But I think I'll wait until summer when the tourists come back."

"Whenever you're ready. So how can we help you?"

"I'd like to take a look at the archives if you don't mind." Maggie pointed a finger toward the ceiling. The archives were housed in an old apartment upstairs.

"Are you researching the women of the quilt blocks?" Adrian asked. "That's going to be a killer story." He pulled out his notepad. "Anything new to report?"

Thad jabbed a thumb at Adrian. "Best thing I ever did was hire this guy. Readership and subscriptions are way up with his local features, so ad revenues are up too." He winked.

"Everyone I've talked to has certainly been impressed," Maggie said. She turned to Adrian. "And I did find the descendant of one of the Sarahs—Sarah Jane Mackenzie. She was the great-aunt of Ruby Adams, who lives out on Parker Road."

Adrian diligently scribbled this down while Thad looked on proudly. "Do you think she was also Mackenzie's Sarah?" Adrian asked.

"I don't know yet. Ruby is looking for a picture of her great-aunt for us to compare. We also found what we think is a picture of the quilting group at the lighthouse today." She pulled out her phone and scrolled to the pictures. Both men came to the front desk to peer at it, Thad adjusting his reading glasses.

"Cool," Adrian said. "Another connection between the quilting blocks and the lighthouse. Think Sarah Monroe is in the picture?"

"She is, but we don't know which woman she is. The names are in alphabetical order, not in the order they're seated. See?" She pulled up her image of the photograph's back and zoomed in on the list of names.

The young reporter snapped his fingers in disappointment. "I guess that would have been too easy."

"Think we can get a copy of the actual photo?" Thad asked. "It will duplicate better for the paper. Although we can work with your digital files in a pinch."

"We'll have to call the Coast Guard. The society wants a copy too."

"Oh, I'll make the call if you want," Adrian said. "I was planning to interview the Coast Guard about the lighthouse anyway."

"That'd be great." Maggie checked the wall clock. "I'd better get upstairs and do my research before you close." The paper closed at four in the winter.

"Go on up," Thad said. "You remember how it's set up."

"Need any help?" Adrian asked.

"Thanks, but I'll be fine. I usually am, right, Thad?"

Thad returned to his desk, pushing his glasses up on his nose as he settled into his seat. "Right. You hold the record for the most visits up there." He grinned. "This makes two." As he began to type, he called, "By the way, I've actually turned on the heat."

"Thank goodness!" Maggie called as she headed for the stairs. *Another sign of increased prosperity*, she thought as she opened the door to the stairwell. At the top, she crossed a small hallway and entered the former living room of an old apartment, which was now the home of the archives. Metal racks stacked with boxes filled the space, a year's worth of issues inside each box. The scent of old dust and paper in the room was strong, but it was an odor Maggie actually enjoyed because of its association with historical research. Each box held a treasure trove of stories concerning life in Somerset Harbor, and she was eager to learn more about the missing heiress and the other women behind the quilt blocks.

Following dates in reverse order, she found the late 1800s in the corner at the back, near a grimy window. According to the box dates, the paper had been founded in 1875, or at least that's where the archives began. Maggie moved along the shelving, glancing at dates: 1888 . . . 1891 . . . 1895. There it was—1898. She pulled the box from the shelf, carried it to a table, and opened the lid. The stack of newspapers was yellow and brittle, the ink faded to brown.

Maggie carefully removed the January papers one by one, handling them gently so they wouldn't crumble. The first February issue was dated February 2, 1898, since the paper came out on Wednesdays. She unfolded it and scanned the front page, then leafed through, looking for any reference to Sarah Monroe's disappearance. Of course a story like that would be front-page news.

She set that issue aside and retrieved the following week's, then the one after that. As she unfolded the third paper, dated February 16, 1898, she noticed something strange. Part of the front page was missing, excised neatly as though someone had used a utility blade. Maybe it was a coincidence. Someone had just happened to clip a story from the only issue left in the archives. The knot in Maggie's belly told her otherwise, though. A scan through the remaining February issues confirmed her theory.

Every story that might have discussed Sarah Monroe's disappearance was gone.

"How's it going up here?"

Maggie turned to see Adrian in the doorway. "Not good, actually." She gestured. "Come see this."

He sauntered to the table and studied the newspapers lined up in a row. "What am I looking at?"

"February 1898 is when Sarah Monroe disappeared. You would think that would be a front-page story for the local paper, right?"

Adrian nodded in agreement. "Of course. It might be the biggest story in a hundred years."

"Well, I can't find a single reference to Sarah. I think someone cut out all the stories." Maggie flipped through the pages showing Adrian the neatly cut holes.

He rubbed his chin thoughtfully, cupping his elbow with the other arm. "Hmm. That is really strange. You would think a complete copy would have been put in the archives."

"Has anyone else been up here lately?" Maggie knew her question sounded odd, but the tightening knot in her belly told her she was on the right track.

"I don't think so. Let's go ask Thad. No, scratch that. Let me get him up here." Adrian pulled out his cell and called downstairs. Through the floorboards, Maggie heard the telephone ring in the newspaper office and the rumble of Thad's deep voice as he answered.

Adrian explained the situation, and a moment later, Thad's footsteps slowly trudged up the stairs. "What's the emergency in the archives?" he asked. "It better be good to make me climb stairs." He flapped the front of his flannel shirt as if out of breath.

"Missing articles," Maggie said succinctly, repeating the show-and-tell.

He, too, appeared puzzled. "They must have been that way for years. No one else has been up here since the last time you and Liz Young were here, Maggie."

Adrian gasped. Maggie and Thad stared at him. "Sorry, but I just thought of something. Thad, remember how the back door was open yesterday? You thought I hadn't closed the door properly, which might have happened since it sticks. But maybe someone broke in."

Thad regarded the younger man over his glasses. "Adrian, I told you I wasn't mad about that. I've done it myself."

Adrian's cheeks flushed. "But I swear I double-checked the door when I left. Someone must have broken in."

Maggie had an inspiration that might clear up the situation and solve her problem at the same time. "You guys have a clippings file, right? Where you keep the stories that might be needed as reference again?"

Thad turned to her. "That's right, we do. Let's go down and see if we have one on Sarah Monroe. Should have thought of that earlier instead of making you muck around up here." He gazed around. "I forget how dusty and gloomy it is up here."

After packing up the loose papers and replacing the box on the shelf, the trio filed out. Downstairs, he let Maggie into the employees-only area behind the counter—which gave her a little thrill—and stopped at the file cabinet holding the clippings files. Opening a drawer marked I–P, he expertly flipped through the files, once, twice, three times. "That's odd. We don't have a file on Sarah Monroe. And I know we ran a retrospective on the centennial of her death in 1998."

"You game to go back up to the archives, Maggie?" Adrian asked.

"Sure," she agreed, but inwardly she knew the relevant

stories from the retrospective would also be missing. And she would hate to be right.

· · · · · · · · · · · · · · · · ·

"So *all* the stories about Sarah Monroe were missing from the archives?" June asked. "That is really strange." June and Maggie were drinking orange-spiced black tea at Carriage House Antiques while planning the next group of displays for after Valentine's Day. June knew a source of antique Irish lace, so they were exploring an Irish cottage theme for St. Patrick's Day.

"It *is* very strange," Maggie said. "I can't imagine why anyone would care if we read those old stories. Now I really want to see them. I wish I could find other copies of the *Herald*." She took a sip from her mug. "Yum. I love this tea."

"It's a special blend I buy at a store here in town," June said. She frowned into the distance. "We don't have any old *Heralds* at the historical society, unfortunately. Maybe we should start doing that. There might be copies at the Maine State Library in Augusta, but that's a haul."

"Do you ever see them for sale? Maybe someone around here collected them."

June's eyes brightened. "I haven't, but I know Jed Parker sells collectible paper items like postcards, tourist brochures, and newspapers. Why don't you give him a call?"

"Jed of Jed's Junk? I saw that place when I went to visit Ruby." Maggie picked up her phone and searched for Jed's number. "The name looked pretty accurate—that's all I'll say."

"Don't let the mess fool you. He's got some good stuff mixed in there. By the way, did you have any luck with Ruby?"

Maggie dialed Jed's number. "We didn't even get around to talking about Ruby's antiques. Hang on a minute and I'll tell you about it."

June swirled the remains of the tea in her mug. "I think I'll make another cup. Want one?" She headed for the back room.

"Sure." Maggie paced back and forth while the phone rang.

"Jed's," a man barked.

Maggie explained who she was and what she was looking for.

"*The Somerset Harbor Herald?* When did that get to be so popular?"

"What do you mean?"

"It's just that you're the second call I've had about it today. And I'll tell you what I told the other person—come on over and look. I have a stack of 'em, not exactly sure what dates. Late 1800s, I know that much. Bought a trunkful at an estate sale."

A sense of urgency rose up inside Maggie. Someone else was scouting out copies of the *Herald*. Could it be related to the missing articles at the newspaper office?

"I'll be right over. See you then." Maggie thanked Jed and hung up.

June slid a fresh mug of tea onto the counter in front of Maggie. "Does he have any?"

Maggie took a hasty sip. "A trunkful, he said. But someone else wants them too."

June frowned. "That's weird."

"It certainly is. I'd better get going before the other person scoops me." Maggie drank half her tea and set down the mug. "Thanks for the tea. I'll have some more when I get back." She hurried to the coat rack, pulled down her jacket, and shrugged into it.

"Oh, Maggie, I meant to tell you. The lighthouse committee is having an impromptu dinner meeting at the Lobster Quadrille tonight. Can you come?"

"I'd love to. Text me the time. I'll see you then, if I don't make it back to the store this afternoon."

Maggie drove out to Parker Road as fast as she dared on the narrow, slippery roads. When she caught herself exceeding the speed limit, she forced herself to let up on the gas, imagining Robert Linton's reaction if he stopped her and she told him she was on the trail of ancient newspapers.

Out at Jed's, a familiar car sat next to the snow-covered humps of Jed's vehicles and other undetermined objects—Mackenzie Floyd's little sedan. Was Mackenzie the one looking into Sarah Monroe? In that case, they could share the articles . . . unless Mackenzie was the one who'd broken into the newspaper office. She didn't live too far from the paper.

Maggie shook off this ridiculous notion and hurried inside, following a beaten track through the otherwise deep snow. Jed apparently took a casual approach to making his store welcoming to visitors. Or maybe he was trying to give people the sense that they were the only ones to find him and his treasures.

To the right of the entrance, a burly man with a big red beard, wearing a John Deere cap, flannel shirt, and jeans, sat at a desk behind a wide counter buried in papers and objects. Among the jumble, Maggie spotted a stereoscope viewer, a stained glass lamp, a rack of vintage postcards, and an antelope skull. Warm air gusted from a potbellied woodstove in the middle of the room. An old basset hound lounged beside the fire, jowly head on its paws.

The man looked up from his paperwork. "Mornin'."

"Good morning. I'm looking for Jed." Maggie approached the counter, skirting an antique wooden machine that promised to x-ray your feet for the best-fitting shoes.

"You found him." Jed stood and moved to the counter, leaning forward on his meaty paws. He pointed at the dog. "And that's Bessie." Bessie raised her head with a jingle of tags. "What can I do for you?"

"Nice to meet you both. I'm Maggie Watson, from Carriage House Antiques. I called earlier about the *Herald* copies."

"Hi, Maggie," called a cheerful voice.

Maggie looked up at the railing guarding the second-floor loft to see Mackenzie peering down. "I thought I saw your car out there."

"Yep, that beater belongs to me." She grinned. "This place is great." She disappeared again.

Jed pointed. "The newspapers are upstairs in the loft, next to the stuffed black bear."

That would be hard to miss. "Thanks." Wondering whether Mackenzie was already looking through the trunk of newspapers, Maggie wound through the crowded room to the wide set of stairs that headed to the second floor. Furniture stood cheek to jowl with bookcases crammed with leather-bound volumes. Long shelves held glassware and lampshades. In one corner hung an array of old farm tools.

At the top of the stairs, Maggie peered around, easily finding the hulking black bear under a skylight that allowed pale winter sunlight to glint off its dense fur. Mackenzie was rummaging through a box nearby.

"Did you find the newspapers?" Maggie called as she picked her way across the loft.

Mackenzie looked confused. "Newspapers?" She held up an empty picture frame. "I'm looking for cheap frames for my paintings and sketches." She showed Maggie another, this one holding a hideous paint-by-number depicting a landscape of woods and stream.

Maggie immediately felt foolish and a little annoyed with herself for jumping to conclusions. "I'm hoping to find some old issues of the *Herald*, with stories about Sarah Monroe." She decided not to mention that those stories were missing from the newspaper's archives. The fewer people who knew about that, the better. She knew how fast news traveled in a small town. Why risk tipping off the real thief?

There was only one trunk sitting near the bear, a black metal storage chest with tarnished silver hardware. Hunkering down, Maggie raised the lid. The interior brimmed with dozens of old newspapers, including not only *The Somerset Harbor Herald* but the *Portland Gazette* as well. The top *Gazette* was dated 1890, so there was a chance, however slight, that she would find the ones she wanted.

With a sigh, she sat down cross-legged on the planks. The willy-nilly way the papers were stacked required her to pull out and look at each one. She was about halfway through when Mackenzie wandered over.

The young woman cocked her head, staring at the bear. "Who on earth would buy one of these? Actually, who would shoot one and have it stuffed? Gruesome." With a shudder, she reached up and stroked the animal's shiny fur. "Huh. It's kind of soft."

"People wear bear coats, or so I've heard."

"Yuck. I'm a faux fur girl myself." Mackenzie regarded the stacks of papers sitting in a semicircle on the floor around Maggie. "Wow. Any luck?"

"Not yet." Maggie pulled out another sheaf of papers. "I'll be here a little longer."

"Do you need me to help?"

"Thanks, but I'm fine."

Mackenzie stood and stretched. "Then I'd better get going. Good luck, and keep me posted."

"I will." Maggie threw her a wave and bent to her task. She had a brief moment of excitement when she spotted January 1898, but there were no issues from that February in the trunk.

After putting the other newspapers back into the trunk—now neatly arranged by title and date for the next customer—Maggie stood, brushing off the seat of her corduroys. "It's all yours," she said to the watching bear.

As she approached the railing on her route back to the stairs, she heard voices and a woman's giggle. Peeking over, she saw Mackenzie talking to Tyler Monroe, their heads mere inches apart. Today Tyler appeared interested in the friendly young woman rather than aloof and dismissive, the opposite of how he'd acted at the lighthouse.

"So it's a date then," Tyler said. "I'll pick you up at seven."

"I'll be ready." Practically glowing, Mackenzie picked up her stack of frames and headed for the door, Tyler leaping ahead to hold it open for her.

"Let me help you with those," he said, following her out.

By the time Maggie got downstairs, both Mackenzie and Tyler's vehicles were headed out of the driveway. Jed stood behind the counter, watching.

"Friend of yours?" he asked. "The young lady, I mean?"

Maggie was puzzled. "Yes. Well, more of an acquaintance, actually. We met a few days ago. Why?"

"Tell her to watch herself." Jed's tone was grim. "Tyler Monroe is . . . well, let's just say he's not the sort of guy I'd want a friend of mine hanging around with."

Alarm jolted Maggie. Had Mackenzie left one bad relationship only to fall into another? "Thanks for the heads-up. I'll try to talk to her. But you know how young people are."

"Sure do. I used to be one, believe it or not. Any luck with what you were looking for?"

Maggie shook her head. "Afraid not. There were a lot of *Herald* issues, but not the ones I need." She had a sudden thought. "You didn't sell any recently, did you?"

Jed leafed through the sales slips on his desk. "Nope," he said after a moment. "Sorry about that. This business is kind of hit or miss."

Maggie mulled over this news, wondering if someone had stolen the papers. If so, there wouldn't be a record of a sale. Or maybe the papers had never been there in the first place. "Thanks anyway. I'll be back out here to look around sometime. You have some very interesting things." That was an understatement.

"So does Carriage House Antiques," he returned politely. "Thanks for coming by."

"Nice meeting you, Jed." Maggie headed for the door but stopped as a sound caught her ear. It was an unusual noise for quiet little Somerset Harbor, where hardly anything happened.

It was the wail of a siren.

Maggie and Jed exchanged startled glances. "A siren? Out here?" Maggie asked.

"Sounds like ambulance or police. I can never tell them apart." Moving fast for such a big man, Jed darted around the corner of the counter toward the front window, joined by Maggie.

A Somerset Harbor ambulance raced along the narrow road, whipping by Jed's property with a flash of lights. Jed ran for his coat, followed by Bessie, her jowls swinging and short legs pumping. "Let's go see what's happening."

Maggie jumped into the passenger seat of Jed's pickup truck. Without question, she squeezed in beside Bessie, reflecting on the intimacy of small-town life. She'd only just met Jed, and now she was riding with him to check out an emergency—it was the neighborly thing to do.

"Who lives down here?" she asked Jed as he turned onto Parker Road and took off after the ambulance, rear tires spinning in the slush. Ruby Adams was the only other resident of the road she knew.

"Only the Moodys, who have a dairy farm, and Ruby Adams. I hope nothing's happened to Ruby. Sweet old gal."

Maggie hoped so too, but as they came around the corner, she saw that the ambulance was indeed parked in Ruby's driveway. In front of it was a car she recognized as Liz Young's.

Jed parked on the side of the road and leaped out. Maggie followed him up the driveway and through the kitchen door. Liz was hovering in the kitchen as EMTs crowded into Ruby's bedroom.

"What's going on, Liz?" Maggie asked.

Liz gestured to a paper bag on the table, which was full of foil containers. "I was delivering Ruby's meals from the Our Daily Bread program when I found her really sick in bed. I think it's the flu."

Maggie released a breath she didn't realize she had been holding. "So she wasn't attacked or anything?"

Her friend gave her a strange look. "Why would you think that?"

"I don't know. Some weird things have been happening." She looked over the silent house. "And Ruby is really isolated out here."

The EMTs moved Ruby onto the gurney and transported her into the kitchen. The elderly woman's eyes were closed, and she looked tiny and frail under her bundle of blankets. Liz reached over and gently squeezed Ruby's shoulder. "Pastor David and I will be praying for you, Ruby."

Maggie touched Ruby's other shoulder. "So will I."

Ruby's eyes flickered open. She raised one hand and tugged on Maggie's sleeve, mumbling something. Maggie bent closer to listen, but when Ruby spoke again, all she could discern was a word beginning with *S*. Maggie shook her head. "Don't try to talk, Ruby. You can tell me when you're feeling better again." She stood back so the EMTs could continue on their way out of the house.

"We're taking her to the hospital if you want to visit later," one of the young men said.

"We will, Ben," Liz said. "Take good care of her."

"You bet, Miz Young."

"Send the bill to me," Jed said. To Maggie and Liz, he said, "I'd better get back to the shop. Coming, Maggie?"

"My car is at Jed's," Maggie explained to Liz. "I was shopping."

"I can give you a ride," Liz said. "But first I want to tidy up around here and make sure everything's locked up before I leave, if that's okay."

"I'll help you. Jed, I'll be back for my car in a bit."

"See you then." With a nod, Jed slipped out the door.

Maggie turned to Liz. "What a nice man he is. So thoughtful and concerned about his neighbor."

"He *is* great. He does a lot for Ruby." Liz looked at the foil-wrapped dinners. "I don't know whether to put those in the fridge or take them back."

"It's hard to know how long she'll be in the hospital, so I wouldn't leave them here. You can always bring her more when she gets home." Maggie headed into the hallway. "Let me check the front door to make sure it's locked." On the way to the door, she shot a casual look into the small sitting room then stopped when she noticed papers and photo albums all over the carpet. Flipped on its side next to them was the cardboard box she'd brought down from the attic at Ruby's request.

Ruby wouldn't have dumped the papers out like that; she was a tidy person, and she treasured old things. What could have happened? Maggie took a step into the room. Maybe she should pick them up.

A floorboard creaked overhead and she halted, shivers running down her spine. Was someone lurking in the house? Had that person scattered the papers? Had Ruby been attacked after all?

"Liz," she croaked. She cleared her throat and tried again, realizing there was no way Liz would have heard her. "Liz? Can you come in here?"

Her friend appeared in the doorway. "What's wrong?"

Maggie pointed to the ceiling and whispered, "I think someone might be upstairs." As if on cue, the boards creaked again.

"That's just the wind," Liz said kindly. "These old houses make all kinds of sounds." She shook her head. "Besides, if there was someone in the house, how did they get here? There aren't any other cars outside."

Tension fled as Maggie realized her friend was right. She was allowing the threatening note and other mysterious events to affect her. "I guess I'm being foolish, but look at this mess. Ruby wouldn't dump out family documents this way." She retrieved the box, then crouched and began to gather the items.

"Maybe she knocked it over by accident." Liz bent to help. "What's their significance anyway?"

"They're old papers that hopefully include information about Sarah Jane Mackenzie, one of the quilt signers. She was Ruby's great-aunt."

Liz's mouth dropped open. "Ruby was trying to say *Sarah* to you in the kitchen."

Maggie paused. "I think you're right." Certainty surged through her. Ruby Adams must have learned something important about her great-aunt.

．．．．．．．．．．．．．．．．．

The golden light streaming from the Lobster Quadrille was like a beacon of cheer on a cold winter night. Maggie locked the car and hurried inside, hungry and tired after her long day. The rustic, seashore-theme restaurant echoed with voices and the clatter of dishes. Savory odors of seafood and hot coffee filled the air.

"I'm with the historical society," Maggie told the hostess, who nodded and led the way to the back of the long, narrow space. Her friends were seated at several small tables pulled together. A buoy-draped net decorated the paneled wall above.

"Hi, Maggie," Ruth said from her seat at the head of the table. "Glad you could make it."

"Me too." Maggie waved. After she slid into the only open chair, between Fran and Ina, she said, "I'm dying for some lobster bisque."

"That is one thing I don't even try to make at The Bean," Daisy said. "I let the chef here take all the honors."

"I just got an update from the hospital," Liz told Maggie from across the table. "Ruby was severely dehydrated, but she's doing much better."

"I'm glad to hear that," Maggie said. "Maybe she'll be up for visitors tomorrow." To the table at large, she said, "Ruby Adams was taken to the hospital today. Liz found her when she was delivering Our Daily Bread meals and called the ambulance."

"Good job, Liz. That's a side benefit of delivering those meals," Daisy said. "We can keep an eye on our clients. A lot of them live alone, and they tend to be older."

"I heard that call," Ina said. "I'm glad the old gal is doing all right." She returned to her menu, seemingly oblivious to the fact that she was about the same age as Ruby.

"Ina, how did you hear the ambulance call?" Fran asked. "Don't tell me you have a police scanner."

"Sure do. My Christmas gift to myself." Ina pursed her lips and continued to study the menu while the others exchanged grins. "Do I want something fried tonight?" She rubbed her midsection. "Might be too late in the day." She slapped the menu down. "I'll stick with the bisque." Ina always had the bisque.

The rest of the group fell silent as they, too, studied the menu and listened to the specials recited by the server, an energetic young woman who reminded Maggie of Mackenzie. After they had placed their orders, Ruth took the floor. "I understand you and Maggie went out to the lighthouse, Ina."

"Yes, we did," Ina said. "Maggie took notes for us regarding what needs to be fixed. Do you have those, Maggie?"

Maggie had found time to type up her notes and print copies early that morning. She passed them around. "The next step is to ask James to look the structure over, or at least point us to someone who can," she said. "This gives us a general idea of the condition of the inside. Outside I think it mainly needs paint."

"They covered the brick with metal at some point," Ina said, "which probably prevented a great deal of deterioration. We should get a stonemason in to look at the foundation, though."

"Good work, ladies," Ruth said. "I move we ask James Bennett to do an initial assessment of the lighthouse."

That motion passed easily, and the conversation turned to fundraising. "Tonight I'd like to get a list of suggestions," Ruth said. "Then we can launch a more formal campaign once we have a concrete goal."

Fran raised her hand tentatively. "I have an idea."

Ruth nodded at the shy shopkeeper. "Go ahead, Fran."

"What if we ask the Oceanview Hotel to dedicate this year's Valentine's dinner to the lighthouse? The manager was in my shop the other day and she said they were having trouble deciding which charity to support. Apparently, most of the local ones have already gotten funds from the Oceanview recently."

"They're great community supporters. That's for sure," Liz Young said. "I say we ask them."

"Any volunteers?" Ruth asked.

There was a short silence before June said, "I'll go over tomorrow. I'll take them the fundraising appeal and explain what we're doing."

"I didn't know you created fundraising materials," Maggie said in surprise. June's resourcefulness never ceased to amaze her.

June pulled a folder out of her tote. "Just one of my many talents," she said with a grin.

"June has helped raise a lot of money for worthy causes," Liz said. "She also helps me with the church appeals." She grinned. "David hates asking for money."

"I don't blame him," Maggie said. "If I were a pastor, I'd rather minister."

June passed around sheets of paper with a nod at Deborah Bennett, who sat quietly at the other end of the table. "Deborah has designed a logo for us to use. Her experience designing quilts has translated very nicely. I think you'll like it."

The fundraising appeal was titled "Save Our Somerset Harbor Lighthouse." The logo was a circle with *SOS* along the top curve, *Lighthouse* along the bottom curve, and a sketch of the lighthouse in the middle.

"Why, this is lovely, Deborah," Daisy said. The other women also exclaimed in delight as Deborah blushed.

"I've written a rough draft, and we can add the amount once we have it," June said. She read the letter aloud.

The society approved June's draft, then paused their meeting when the food when came out of the kitchen, steamy-hot and delicious. Maggie chose a warm yeast roll from the basket, then turned to Fran. "Can you please pass me the butter?"

Fran didn't appear to hear. She was staring straight ahead, her normally pink cheeks ashen. Maggie followed her gaze to the front of the restaurant. Tyler Monroe and Mackenzie Floyd were being shown to a table next to the wall, Tyler chivalrously holding Mackenzie's arm. After he released it, Mackenzie slipped out of her coat, revealing a short black-velvet dress, matching tights, and little black ankle boots trimmed with silver.

Maggie touched Fran's arm. "What's wrong?" she whispered. This was the second time Fran had reacted oddly to Tyler Monroe. At least she assumed it was toward Tyler.

Fran shook her head sharply. "I can't talk about it right now." With a sudden move, she shoved back her chair and got up from the table. She strode briskly across the restaurant, her head firmly turned away from the couple.

"Where's she going in such a hurry?" Ina bent over her bowl and scooped up a spoonful of bisque.

"The ladies' room, I think." Maggie was reluctant to make Fran's evident distress a common topic of conversation.

Tyler and Mackenzie had their heads close together as they studied the menu together. Tyler's arm was draped around the back of Mackenzie's chair. *Very cozy*, Maggie thought.

A young man wearing an apron emerged from the kitchen, carrying a rack of clean glasses in both hands, apparently heading for the bar area at the left side of the room.

Ina dropped her spoon with a clatter and nudged Maggie with her elbow. "Uh-oh. Here comes trouble."

"Is that Cody Becker?" Maggie asked, dreading the answer.

"I believe so," Ina said. "I'd recognize his ugly mug anywhere."

The hair on the back of Maggie's neck stood up. Had he noticed Mackenzie and Tyler?

Her fear was realized. Just as Cody hefted the rack over the bar for unloading, he caught sight of the couple at their table. The rack hit the counter with a crash, drawing attention from many guests, except for Mackenzie and Tyler who were busy gazing into each other's eyes.

Ina threw down her napkin and rose. "I'm going in. Coming?"

Despite her doubts, Maggie followed Ina, hoping that at least she could prevent the older woman from getting hurt, as Cody was three times her size. He was storming across the restaurant, fists clenched; the glare on his face made Maggie think of a bull about to charge.

Maggie glimpsed Mackenzie's startled face, but she was soon distracted by Ina. The older woman had darted into Cody's path, forcing him to halt, and she put one hand on her hip. With the other, she jabbed her forefinger into his broad chest.

"Back off," Ina snarled.

He put his own hands on his hips. "Outta my way, Granny."

Ina refused to move. "Maggie, call the police," she called over her shoulder.

Cody's hands flew up. "What for? I haven't done anything."

"Yet. I think you'd better get back to work and leave Mackenzie alone."

"I just want to talk to her."

"The way you were 'talking' to her the other day?" Ina shook her head vehemently. "No sir."

Patrons nearby had stopped talking. To Maggie, it felt like all eyes were on them. The hostess and the bartender headed their way, looks of concern on their faces.

Glancing around like a trapped animal, Cody realized he had a rapt audience. "This is nuts." He pulled his apron off and wadded it into a ball, then thrust it toward Ina. "I quit." He turned on his heel and stormed out of the room.

Ina handed the apron to the bartender. "I think you need a new dishwasher." Then to Maggie, she said, "Let's get back to our soup before it gets cold."

Maggie saw that Mackenzie was still deep in conversation with Tyler.

Then Maggie thought of Fran. She looked at the hallway leading to the restrooms. Fran still hadn't appeared. "I'll be right there. I'm going to check on Fran."

"Suit yourself." Ina swaggered back toward their table with the panache of a gunslinger who'd just won a shoot-out.

The restrooms only held one person at a time, and the women's room was locked. Maggie knocked.

"I'll be right out," Fran called.

Maggie leaned close to the door, speaking just loudly enough so Fran could hear her. "Fran, it's Maggie. Are you all right?"

Silence. Then, in a tone that surprised Maggie, the normally sweet and calm Fran snapped, "Of course I am. Do you really want details?"

Maggie immediately felt foolish. Fran was indisposed, and she had assumed an emotional upset. "Sorry to intrude. See you back at the table."

Before she could move, the lock turned with a clunk and Fran opened the door a crack. Her eyes were red-rimmed, and she clutched a tissue in her hand. "I'm sorry, Maggie. I know you're trying to be nice. It's just . . ." Her voice trailed off and tears welled in her eyes.

A woman entered the hallway, and Maggie realized they shouldn't tie up the ladies' room. At the end of the hallway was an alcove, a small area that had once held a telephone, Maggie guessed. Now a love seat and a fake tree filled the space.

"Come out here and we'll talk for a minute." Maggie led Fran to the sofa and they sat. Keeping her eyes on the landscape painting on the opposite wall, she gave the other woman time to compose herself.

"You must think I'm a fool," Fran mumbled. "Making a scene like this."

Maggie patted Fran's hand. "Of course not. I'm guessing it was seeing Tyler that upset you?"

Fran nodded, then wiped her eyes again. "I thought I was over him. But then when I saw him in my shop the other day, I realized I wasn't." She sighed deeply. "And then tonight, he saunters in . . ."

"With another woman," Maggie finished the sentence. "It hit you right in the belly."

"Exactly." Fran met Maggie's gaze. "You've been there?"

"I have." It had been a one-sided crush on Maggie's part a long time ago, well before she'd met Richard. But Fran didn't need Maggie's sob story. She needed support and sympathy.

"The thing is," Fran said in a low, confidential tone, "it wasn't a healthy relationship. He was . . . elusive—secretive, even. Left me hanging a lot." Maggie sensed that she wanted to share more but Fran must have reconsidered. "No, it wasn't good for me at all."

"Those hard-to-get types can hook you the worst." Again, Maggie drew on experience from adolescence. Apparently some men and women played the same games as adults. "He's not worthy of your affection."

"You're right." Fran's spine straightened, and a brave little smile broke through the tears. "What do I need Tyler Monroe for?"

"That's the spirit," Maggie said, smiling in return. "Are you ready to head back to the table?" Her stomach grumbled, and she thought of her delicious bisque, probably stone cold by now.

Fran stood and squared her shoulders. "Yes, I am." She lifted her chin. "It's his loss."

Back at the table, Fran appeared to be over her distress as she joined the general conversation and merriment. But Maggie noticed she kept her eyes averted from the couple seated across the room. After hearing about Fran's experience on top of the warning from Jed, Maggie was even more concerned for Mackenzie's well-being. Tyler was handsome, sophisticated, and wealthy, not to mention about ten years Mackenzie's senior. Heady stuff for a young and vulnerable woman trying to make her way in the world alone.

"Any news on the women who signed the quilt blocks, Maggie?" Ruth asked, drawing her attention back to the group.

"I've tracked down one Sarah." Maggie shared with the group that Ruby Adams was likely related to Sarah Jane Mackenzie. "I hope I'll be able to get more information from Ruby once she's better."

"I've found something. Maybe." Deborah Bennett's soft voice

startled everyone. "I decided to look around my attic because I remembered having a few old things my family had passed down through the generations. I found one of the diaries kept by my grandmother, Priscilla Allen."

"She signed one of the blocks." Ina bounced in her chair with excitement. "Did she write anything about Sarah Monroe?"

"I don't know yet. I've just started reading." Deborah laughed softly. "So far there's a lot about the weather, an unpleasant neighbor, and her daughters, Priscilla and Drusilla. Apparently they were quite naughty at times, which is funny because Great-Aunt Drusilla was always quite strict with my mother and then with me."

"Everyone thinks old diaries are full of secrets," Daisy said. "But often they are just plain boring." She winked. "Except for mine, of course."

"So are church records," Liz said with a shrug. "But I'm going to give them a go tomorrow if anyone wants to join me."

"I'll come over," Maggie offered. "I think I've recovered from my last experience with the church records." A few months before, she had been doing research on something else and had gotten trapped for a few harrowing hours in the cellar where the church records were kept.

Liz beamed at her. "Well, I'm certainly not going to leave you down there alone this time."

The server appeared at the table. "Anyone want dessert? We have homemade apple crisp with ice cream. It's fresh from the oven."

Everyone groaned in protest—and ordered dessert and coffee.

Full and content, Maggie headed right to bed when she got home, in a house blessedly free of threatening notes and other unpleasant surprises. Perhaps the patrol car she'd passed on Shoreline Drive had discouraged the mysterious prowler. She sure hoped so.

Curled up in bed with a purring Snickers and a new mystery novel, curtains shut tight against the frosty night, she felt snug and peaceful. Her questions, concerns, and fears could wait until tomorrow, to be faced in the bright light of day.

The telephone rang shortly after midnight, startling her out of a sound sleep into full alertness. She snatched up the phone from her nightstand. Calls in the dead of night were never good news.

"Hello?" She prayed silently.

"Maggie, it's Ina."

Relief whooshed through Maggie at the sound of her friend's voice. That meant the bad news had nothing to do with Emily. But then her stomach tightened. Someone else must be hurt or in trouble for Ina to call. "What—" Her voice was hoarse, so she cleared her throat. "What is it?"

"Mackenzie Floyd was just hit by a car."

12

Maggie gasped in shock at this news, her mind filling with horrible images of Mackenzie lying in the snow, bleeding, even— "Is she all right?"

"I don't know. She's at the hospital." Ina's tone was gruff. Although Maggie didn't know her extremely well, she sensed Ina was struggling to control her own shock and upset over the accident.

"What happened?"

"Hit-and-run while she was crossing the street. That's all I know from the scanner and the little bit Robert would tell me."

Hit-and-run. Cody Becker immediately came to mind. Had he tried to kill Mackenzie? Maggie threw back the covers. "I'll go down to the hospital."

"Can you pick me up?" Ina asked. "I'm kind of fond of that little girl. She has spunk."

Maggie was already rummaging for a pair of jeans and a sweater. "Of course."

The hospital emergency room was fairly quiet as Maggie and Ina entered through the automatic doors. An admitting clerk sat behind the semicircular desk, and several young people were seated in the waiting area, watching television or gazing at their phones. One young man was sleeping curled up on a short vinyl sofa.

"Maggie! Ina!" A young woman rose to her feet. It was Jenny, the waitress from The Busy Bean. "Are you here for Mackenzie?"

"Yes, we are," Maggie said. "How is she?"

Jenny's normally smiling mouth was turned down in a frown of dismay. "Not sure yet. The doctor is supposed to give us an update when he has more details." She gestured to the door marking the entrance to the examining rooms. Jenny glared at the desk clerk. "*She* won't let any of us go back there."

The woman at the desk, middle-aged with a thin face and sandy permed hair, rolled her eyes. "Family only," Jenny intoned.

Maggie and Ina followed Jenny and joined the others in the waiting area, their boots squeaking on the polished tile.

"What happened?" Ina asked Jenny as they sat. "I couldn't get all the details from the police scanner."

Jenny's brows rose at the mention of the scanner, and a young man nearby looked up from his phone. "You have a scanner? Cool."

Ina smiled smugly. "I sure do. So were there any witnesses?"

"We all saw it," Jenny said, gesturing to the other young people in the room. "Mackenzie was hit by a white pickup in front of The Whale's Tooth when she was crossing the street." Shuddering, she put both hands over her face. "It was horrible."

"The Whale's Tooth?" Maggie had seen the place, a pizza-and-sandwich joint on one of the side streets downtown. "It didn't happen at the Quadrille?"

Another girl, a pretty blonde, spoke. "No, she came over to join us after dinner." She blinked back tears. "She was bragging about her hot date."

"And playing a killer game of pool," the boy added.

Maggie was silently relieved Mackenzie's date with Tyler hadn't extended past dinner. "So what exactly happened?"

"We stayed until closing," Jenny said. "Midnight. Then Mackenzie and I were going to walk home together. But I was talking for a minute with Ben,"—she pointed to the young man with the phone—"and Mackenzie started to cross the street by herself."

"The truck came out of nowhere." The blonde girl took up

the story, perching on the edge of her seat. "Mackenzie was in the middle of the street. She had no time to get out of the way."

"It knocked her down, and she hit her head really hard." Tears rolled down Jenny's cheeks, and the other girl put her arm around her.

"I don't think the lights were on," Ben added. "I sure didn't see it coming."

Maggie and Ina exchanged glances. By the grim look on the older woman's face, Maggie guessed that Ina was thinking what she was thinking—that the hit-and-run had been a deliberate attempt on Mackenzie's life.

The hospital entrance doors whooshed, and Robert Linton entered. He headed straight for the desk, where he had a low-voiced conversation with the attendant. Then he came over to the group.

"Do you know anything, officer?" Jenny asked, her eyes hopeful.

"No more than you do, I'm afraid," Robert said. His gaze fell on Maggie and Ina. "What are you two doing here?"

"Holding vigil, just like the rest of Mackenzie's friends," Ina said. By the determined expression on Ina's face, Maggie guessed she was about to share their theory of the "accident."

Before Ina could say anything more, Maggie jumped in. "Can we speak to you in private, Robert?" Mackenzie's friends didn't need to hear that the incident might have been intentional. That juicy piece of information would be all over town in a minute, which might hinder the investigation.

Robert reached up and shoved his hat back, scratching his head. "I suppose so. I just came down here to check on Miss Floyd's condition."

"We'll just need a minute," Ina said. "Believe me, it's important."

"I suppose I have time for a coffee," Robert said and gave his aunt a small smile. The cafeteria was closed, so he led the way to a vending area down the hall, next to another small waiting room.

While Robert fed coins into the coffee machine, Ina said, "We think that driver hit Mackenzie on purpose."

Robert pushed one of the buttons and hot liquid began to stream into a paper cup. "Aunt Ina." His voice was deliberately patient. "I understand that you're upset about the accident. But there is no evidence that it was anything but that. We are investigating carefully."

""But we have good reason to think she was hit on purpose. Remember Cody Becker?" Maggie asked.

Robert picked up the cup, took a sip, and grimaced. "Oh yeah, the boyfriend."

"The *ex*-boyfriend. Who was shaking her like this, right in broad daylight." Ina demonstrated. "That's abuse."

"It's a long way from shaking someone to running them down," Robert said, his tone still maddeningly calm. He took another tentative sip of coffee and made a face; apparently the brew was lackluster at best.

"Maybe so. But Cody saw Mackenzie tonight with another man. He almost busted up the Quadrille." Maggie gestured toward Ina. "If it hadn't been for your aunt, there might have been bloodshed."

Ina preened at this acknowledgement of her talent in defusing situations. "Well, maybe not bloodshed, but an ugly scene for sure."

Robert sighed, set down his coffee on a nearby table, and pulled out his notebook. "All right. Tell me what happened."

Maggie and Ina took him through the situation at the Quadrille. "I think we should find out whether Cody Becker drives a white truck," Maggie concluded. "It sounds to me like he could have been lurking outside The Whale's Tooth, waiting for an opportunity to catch Mackenzie alone."

"A truck driving without lights." Ina tapped her nose. "Surely that is suspicious behavior."

"The headlights weren't on?" By Robert's raised brows, Maggie guessed this was news to him. "I'd better question those kids again, see what else they remember."

Maggie turned as Jenny appeared in the doorway. "Any news?" Maggie asked. Her heart crept into her throat as she waited for Jenny's response.

Jenny broke into a bright smile. "She's going to be all right. The doctor said it's just a minor concussion."

After spending a few minutes celebrating with the others and making plans to see Mackenzie in the morning, when she would be allowed to have visitors, Maggie took Ina home.

Ina gave a huge yawn as Maggie pulled into her driveway. "I'm pooped. Tonight was more than enough excitement for an old lady."

"I'm exhausted too," Maggie said. "But mainly relieved that Mackenzie is going to be all right." Every muscle in her body ached, and she couldn't wait to crawl in beside Snickers again. Hopefully he'd kept the bed warm for her.

Ina paused with her hand on the door handle. "I sure hope the police get the lead out of their shorts and find that truck. I don't see Cody giving up just because he failed this time."

Dread iced Maggie's core. She had been so focused on the happy ending to the incident that she hadn't thought about Mackenzie still being in danger, which she would be as long as Cody Becker was free. "I guess we'll have to stay on them. Good night, Ina." She waited until Ina made it inside before backing out of the driveway.

Only one or two lights were on in the quiet houses she passed. The sky was clear, and she could see broad swatches of glittering stars in the inky sky. The serene sight made her sigh, peace stealing into her weary bones. How beautiful Somerset Harbor was, even in the bleak midwinter.

As she passed a side street, headlights flashed on and a vehicle pulled out behind her. *Another late-night traveler or very early riser.* Maggie continued to drive cautiously along the street, not wanting to hit a patch of ice.

The headlights drew closer, and since the other vehicle was much taller than her little Jetta, they shone right into Maggie's mirrors, blinding her.

Maggie adjusted the rearview and the side mirrors so she could see. Gingerly hitting the gas, she sped up a few miles per hour, hoping to pull away from the inconsiderate motorist.

The other driver kept pace, maintaining a distance of mere inches behind her rear bumper. If she had to stop suddenly, he would definitely hit her.

Maggie's heartbeat sped up. There was something ominous about the headlights and grille looming behind her, like a monster on her tail. Her hands began to sweat inside her gloves. Should she drive to the police station? There was nothing else open this late. But no, she had no way to prove she was being followed, and she didn't want to seem like a hysterical female. She'd told the police about similar incidents before, and they were never overly concerned. Surely this was nothing.

Maggie took the route back to Sedgwick Manor. When she reached the foot of her driveway, she turned in with a sudden yank at the wheel, the rear of the car fishtailing. Then she gunned it up the driveway, intent on reaching safety.

To her relief, the other vehicle kept going on the main road. As it passed under a streetlight, she gasped. It was a white pickup truck.

By the time she got inside, locked the doors, and climbed back into bed with the snoozing Snickers, she had convinced herself that she had overreacted. How many pickups were there in the area, anyway? Just about every tradesman had one. Surely it had been another late-night traveler.

At least, that's what she told herself.

· · · · · · · · · · · · · · · · ·

The small hospital was a different place in the light of day, bustling with medical personnel, patients, and visitors despite its small size and limited services. Maggie stopped at the main reception desk and learned Mackenzie was in room 210 before taking the elevator to the second floor.

"Which way is room 210?" she asked the nurse at the station on the second floor.

The young woman, not much older than Mackenzie, tossed her ponytail as she looked up from her computer. "You here to see Mackenzie Floyd?" At Maggie's nod, she pointed down the hallway to the right. "Three doors down. Just follow the smell of roses." She beamed. "Someone has a very attentive boyfriend."

Maggie followed her directions, puzzled. *Attentive boyfriend?* Surely Cody Becker wasn't here in the hospital. Her steps quickened. What if he had used roses to gain access and was planning to hurt her again? Why hadn't the police posted a guard for the victim of a hit-and-run? *Oh, right, they think it was an accident.*

Maggie burst through the open door into the room. Bemused, she had to blink a few times before the scene in front of her made sense. The room was filled with a few bouquets of red roses. But it was Tyler Monroe sitting beside Mackenzie's bed, holding her hand tenderly.

"Maggie!" Mackenzie's eyes were bright. "How nice of you to come visit me." Tyler nodded a greeting but didn't budge from her side.

Maggie attempted a smile. "Of course. I was concerned about you. How are you feeling?"

Mackenzie put her hand to her head, touching a white bandage lightly. "I'm okay. Still have a headache."

"When are they going to let you out of here, princess?" Tyler asked.

Mackenzie started to shake her head then stopped, wincing. "I don't know. The nurse said the doctor will come by soon and tell me."

Tyler shifted his chair a little closer to the bed, and Maggie stood in the middle of the floor, feeling like a third wheel. "Maybe I'll come back later," she said.

Tyler nodded.

"Please stay." The pleading note in Mackenzie's voice won Maggie over, but to placate Tyler, she approached the closest bouquet of roses and bent to sniff them. "Wow. These are lovely."

"I bought out the shop," Tyler told her. "They weren't too happy since Valentine's Day is in a few days. But hey, nothing's too good for her." At the last statement, Tyler gazed at Mackenzie with a devotion that made Maggie uncomfortable.

The mention of Valentine's Day also reminded Maggie that she still hadn't talked to James, but she pushed the thought out of her mind.

"Oh, Tyler. You're so good to me." Mackenzie sounded breathless, like the vulnerable young woman she was.

"Of course I am. You deserve it."

Out of the corner of her eye, Maggie saw Tyler lift Mackenzie's hand to his lips. Instead of swooning, Maggie felt rather nauseated. He was coming on a bit too strong for her taste.

Before she could think of a way to gracefully extricate herself, a short, thin, balding man bustled into the room, followed by a nurse. "How are you doing today, Mackenzie?" He approached the bedside, ushering Tyler out of the way.

"I'm all right, Dr. Simons. My head still hurts."

"Her vitals were good this morning," the nurse said.

Dr. Simons checked Mackenzie's vitals again. Then he stood and considered her for a moment, thinking. Finally he said, "I think it's fine for you to go home."

"Yay!" Mackenzie beamed, moving as if to slide out of bed.

"But," the doctor added, holding up a hand, "you cannot be alone today."

Mackenzie's face fell. "Darn it. Jenny and the girls are working."

Tyler opened his mouth to say something, but Maggie got there first. "She can come home with me." When Dr. Simons turned to consider her, she added, "I'm Maggie Watson. I don't have to be anywhere today." *Goodbye, church records. Sorry, Liz.* "I know what to watch for. My daughter got a concussion once while playing field hockey."

That piece of information appeared to seal the deal. "You can go, Mackenzie, if you stay with Mrs. Watson for the next twenty-four hours."

"Are you sure, Maggie?" Mackenzie bit her lip. "I don't want to be any trouble."

"That's right, Maggie. Surely you need to tend your business?" Tyler's tone was silky, but Maggie heard steel underneath.

"Actually I don't. My store manager can take care of everything for the next day or so. She's managed without me before."

Dr. Simons looked puzzled, so Maggie explained. "I own Carriage House Antiques."

"Oh yes. My wife loves that place. Esther Simons."

Esther was a regular customer. "Oh yes. I know your wife." Maggie held out her hand toward the doctor. "Nice to meet you. She often speaks of you and your sons."

"Good to meet you too." The doctor shook her hand, then said to the nurse, "I'll write up the discharge papers."

"Great." The nurse looked at Tyler, then Maggie. "Let's give Mackenzie some privacy to get dressed, shall we?"

. . . .

"Wow, I can't believe this house." Mackenzie kept up the refrain of admiration and awe all the way up the driveway, through the foyer with its crystal chandelier, and into the library, which Maggie had decided was a good place for Mackenzie to relax.

"Take a seat and I'll light a fire," Maggie said. She went to the fireplace and began to pile up kindling and crumpled newspaper on the hearth.

"Look at all these books." Mackenzie gazed around at the floor-to-ceiling bookcases, the high shelves accessed with a rolling library ladder. "Have you read all of them?"

"Not even a fraction. I inherited this house from my aunt recently. So it will be a while."

Snickers came running into the room, immediately diverting from his path toward Maggie to jump up beside Mackenzie on the sofa. He reached out an inquiring nose, sniffing her as she tentatively touched his head. "He's adorable. What's his name?"

Maggie added a couple of logs to the pile. "That's Snickers. He likes chin scratches and belly rubs." She lit the fire with a long match, enjoying the crackle of flames as the paper and then the kindling caught.

"I love sitting in front of a fire," Mackenzie said. Snickers had rolled onto his back, and she stroked his fluffy tummy gently. The cat purred loudly and closed his eyes.

"Me too. I was just about to make some lunch. How does tomato soup and grilled cheese sound?"

"Awesome. That's my favorite." Mackenzie shifted as though to rise.

"My daughter's too," Maggie said as she held up her hand. "No, you stay here and rest. We can eat in here." She gave the fire a poke to make sure the logs would burn evenly and headed out to the kitchen. Snickers didn't follow. He was having too much fun with his new friend.

As she walked toward the kitchen, Maggie's cell phone rang.

"Good morning—well, afternoon, Ina. How are you?"

"Fine, thanks. Heard you took our patient home with you."

Maggie was always amazed at how fast news traveled in Somerset Harbor. "Yes I did. What, was it on the scanner?" she teased. She opened the fridge and pulled out cheese and butter for the sandwiches.

"Ha ha," Ina replied sarcastically. "Of course not. But I did hear something else from the police."

Maggie retrieved a can of tomato soup from the pantry. "What's that?"

"Cody Becker couldn't have run over Mackenzie. He was arrested two hours earlier in Pelican Cove. Driving under the influence at the wheel of a Chevy hatchback."

After disconnecting with Ina, Maggie continued to prepare lunch on autopilot; her mind was buzzing with the mystery of who had been at the wheel of the white pickup.

Maybe the hit-and-run had been an accident after all. Mackenzie couldn't have been targeted on purpose; who other than Cody would want to hurt such a sweet girl? Relief loosened the muscles in her neck, and Maggie gave a huge, gusty sigh. She had been more worried than she had realized.

Thank goodness Mackenzie's ex-boyfriend hadn't escalated his abuse with a murder attempt. Too bad the police couldn't keep him in jail for a while. He was probably already out on bail.

Maggie transferred the crusty brown sandwiches to plates and cut them in half diagonally, the way Emily liked. As she was reaching for two bowls to hold the bubbling soup, her phone chimed again. Not really wanting to take a call, she checked the caller ID anyway.

It was Adrian Diaz, the reporter from the *Herald*. Out of curiosity, she answered. After a brief exchange of pleasantries, Adrian said, "Maggie, I'm out at the lighthouse with the Coast Guard. I can't find the photograph you were talking about."

"The one of the quilting group? It should be right next to a '60s Polaroid of three kids in front of the lighthouse."

"I'm looking right at the Polaroid, but I don't see the other photograph. I've even looked on the floor to make sure it didn't fall down."

"We did take it down to examine and photograph it, but I made sure it was securely back in place afterward." Now the photograph was gone too? Had Tyler Monroe snatched it on his way out? It did depict his famous ancestor, after all.

"I suppose we can use the digital shots you took, but I'd rather have the real thing," Adrian said.

"Let me ask the people who were with me. Maybe one of them knows where it is." Ina and Mackenzie would be easy to question, but Maggie didn't relish approaching Tyler Monroe with such a question. She had a feeling the businessman wouldn't take well to basically being accused of theft. She hoped the photo would turn up and she wouldn't have to ask him.

"The good news," Adrian said, "is that they're letting me borrow a bunch of these photographs so I can do a two-page spread about the lighthouse through the years. If I get copies made, does the society want a set? Maybe you can use them in your materials or in a display."

"That would be wonderful, Adrian. Thanks." Maggie could already picture a portable exhibit, one they could take to various fundraising events to save the lighthouse. On that positive note, Maggie hung up and finished preparing lunch.

. . . .

"This is delicious." Mackenzie eagerly spooned up the creamy tomato soup.

Maggie was gratified to see her injured guest display a hearty appetite. They each had their own tray table, and Snickers bounced between Maggie and Mackenzie in hopes of being fed a tidbit. He loved cheese in any form.

"When do you think we can visit Ruby Adams?" Mackenzie asked.

"Oh, right, I haven't had a chance to tell you. She's in the hospital."

A look of concern crossed Mackenzie's face. "Oh no! What happened?"

"She came down with the flu and got dehydrated." Maggie felt a pang of remorse. In the excitement about Mackenzie's accident, she hadn't spared a thought for Ruby and her illness. She should have visited her that morning, when she'd been at the hospital anyway. "Let me make a call and see how she's doing." She moved her meal tray out of the way.

"I hope she's all right." Mackenzie stirred her soup.

"Me too." Maggie retrieved her phone from the kitchen and dialed Liz.

Liz picked right up. "Hey, friend, I was wondering when I'd see you at the church office today."

Maggie explained the situation with Mackenzie. "I'll come down tomorrow or the next day, if that's all right."

"Sounds good. Those records aren't going anywhere."

"I was also wondering about Ruby Adams. How is she doing?"

Mackenzie was watching Maggie as if she were trying to decipher the side of the conversation she couldn't hear. Snickers, who had settled on Mackenzie as the best candidate for affection and treats, rolled over and butted her thigh with his head as if to say, "Don't forget about me!" Mackenzie reached down and stroked his throat.

"She is doing really well, I'm happy to report. They're taking her home today."

Maggie thought about Ruby's isolated home and the mysterious intruder who had searched through her papers. "Ruby won't be alone, I hope."

"Oh no. She'll have constant home care for a while."

"Good. If you speak to her, tell her I'll be over to see her as soon as she's up to it." She winked at Mackenzie. "I have someone I want her to meet."

Mackenzie pumped a fist and mouthed, "Yes!"

The two women spent the afternoon relaxing, something

Maggie realized she hadn't done much of lately. Mackenzie read a book and sketched for a while, then took a nap in front of the fire with Snickers snuggled up beside her. Maggie puttered around the house, doing laundry, getting Emily's room ready for Mackenzie, and preparing a savory homemade chicken pie for supper. That was another of Emily's favorites, and there was no better comfort food on a blustery winter night.

When dinner was ready, Maggie crept into the library, not wanting to startle Mackenzie if she was still snoozing.

Mackenzie was sitting up, sketching. She peeped over her shoulder and spotted Maggie. "Come see what I drew for you."

The young artist had sketched Snickers curled up in a ball, tail touching his nose and one eye open. "It's beautiful." Maggie was touched by Mackenzie's talent and thoughtfulness. "I'll frame this and hang it up."

Mackenzie blushed. "It's the least I can do to repay you for your hospitality."

"Oh, no payment necessary." Maggie set the sketch in a safe place on a table. "If you're up to it, I thought we would eat in the kitchen."

After dinner, Mackenzie went up to bed, and Maggie decided to work on her notes about the quilt blocks. She pulled out her notepad and went into the cozy office where her late aunt had managed the antiques business, and sat behind the beautiful partners' desk.

She began to look over the list of women who had stitched the blocks. They knew a bit about some of them already. Sarah Jane Mackenzie was related to Ruby Adams. She hoped she and Liz would find Sarah Anne Stewart in the marriage archives. Nellie Linton was Ina's grandmother, and Priscilla Allen was Deborah Bennett's grandmother.

Again her thoughts turned to the mystery of Julia Sedgwick's involvement. Maybe her assumption that Julia had worked on the quilt was wrong, although she was in the picture of the group and the blocks had been found here, in this house.

But Fran thought there was a missing square—

Tap, tap.

Maggie's head jerked up. *What was that?*

Tap, tap.

Someone—or something—was outside the office window. Maggie took a deep, shuddering breath. It was probably just a branch blowing in the wind.

Tap, tap came again, too regular and firm to be the movement of a branch. Feeling as if she had been dropped into a nightmare, Maggie tiptoed to the window and stood out of view as she pulled aside the long drape. All she could see was a reflection of the office in the window. Although she waited long minutes, nothing stirred in the winter night.

· · · · · · · · · · · · · · · · ·

In the bright light of morning, Maggie found it hard to believe that she had let a random noise scare her so much. Feeling slightly foolish, she put on her coat and boots and trudged around the house. She started when she saw footprints near the window, but then she realized there were a couple of different sizes and shapes overlapping each other. Nate Gregory had come out to knock down icicles off the roof yesterday with his crew. With a shrug, she decided to chalk the whole thing up to nerves.

A little later, sitting in the sunny breakfast nook, drinking coffee and enjoying poached eggs on toast with Mackenzie, she realized how nice it was to have a young person in the house. At times like this, she really missed her daughter. Shoving aside empty-nest thoughts, she said, "You're looking much better today, Mackenzie."

"I feel a lot better. No headache." Mackenzie's smiling face reflected the resilience of youth's rapid healing ability. "I can't believe the doctor wants me to take another day off."

"I can. Besides, Snickers likes having you around."

Mackenzie reached out and stroked the cat sitting on the window cushion between them. "I like him too."

"So take it easy today. Do some reading and drawing. I have to run a few errands, but I'll have my cell if you need me." Maggie hesitated then. She hated to spoil the cheerful mood with fearful talk, but she had to warn Mackenzie. "Please keep the doors locked, okay? As a matter of fact, don't even answer the door. I don't want Cody Becker to bother you." Maybe he hadn't been driving the pickup truck, but he had been angry about Mackenzie's date with Tyler.

"Cody?" Mackenzie's eyes widened. "I don't think he even knows where I am."

"You never know, someone might have told him. If I've learned one thing living in this town, it's that news travels fast."

Mackenzie regarded Maggie steadily, with a small smile playing around her lips that looked suspiciously like the one Emily often wore when she was humoring her mother. "I'm not worried about Cody, but it's your place, so whatever you say goes, of course."

Maggie patted Mackenzie's hand. "Let's just say I don't like the cut of Cody's jib, as the old-timers say." In addition to Cody, there was the person who had left the threatening note to worry about, as well as the strange man who had watched her and Mackenzie leave the historical society meeting.

And according to Jed, Ina, and nearly everyone else she'd talked to about him, Tyler Monroe was a problem too. Should she say something? Warning Mackenzie away from a man she liked—particularly a rich one who doted on her—would probably go over like a lead balloon, if similar experiences with her daughter were any indication. Realizing she was being a little cowardly, she decided to leave that discussion for later. With any luck, the fledgling romance would fizzle.

Getting up from the table, Maggie said, "If anyone bothers you, anyone at all, call me. I won't be gone long."

Mackenzie grinned. "Don't worry. We'll be fine." She chucked the cat under his chin. "Won't we, Snickers?"

Hoping she was doing the right thing by leaving the young woman alone, Maggie gathered her things and drove downtown. She stopped by the bank to make a deposit and picked up a few items at the grocery store. Being out and about, greeting neighbors, and experiencing the friendly hustle and bustle of town lifted the sense of foreboding that had been hovering over her like a cloud.

On the way home, she decided to swing into The Busy Bean and pick up some cookies. She could use another cup of coffee too. The first person she saw inside was Fran, standing at the counter, purchasing a coffee to go.

"Hey, Maggie. Do you have a minute? I want to go over my plan for the restoration of the quilt blocks."

"Sure. I'll take a large coffee to go," she told Jenny, who was working the counter. "And a dozen assorted cookies." Today Daisy had cranberry–white chocolate, ginger–chocolate chip, and sugar-sprinkled molasses.

"Four of each?" At Maggie's nod, Jenny picked up a piece of wax paper and opened the case. "How's Mackenzie doing?"

"She's much better. I think she'll be back to work tomorrow if the doctor says it's okay."

"We sure could use her." Jenny slid the last cookie into a white bag and set it on the counter. "We've been swamped." She poured Maggie a coffee to go.

Maggie leaned over the counter and lowered her voice. "You haven't seen Cody Becker around, have you?"

"You mean Mackenzie's ex?" Jenny shook her head as she rang up the sale. "No, thank goodness."

"Good. If you do, don't tell him where she's staying, all right?"

"I won't. I don't like that guy." Jenny handed Maggie the receipt.

Fran and Maggie walked across the street together. "It's nice of you to take Mackenzie in," Fran said as they trooped over a snowbank to the front door of the quilt shop. She rummaged around in her parka pocket and pulled out her keys.

"I guess I feel kind of protective toward her," Maggie said. "She reminds me of my daughter."

Fran didn't say anything else as she unlocked the door and led the way into the shop, stepping aside to let Maggie enter before removing the Back Soon sign from the door.

"Wow. The shop looks great." Maggie changed the subject, guessing that Fran didn't want to talk about Tyler Monroe, and continuing to speak of Mackenzie might lead there. She wasn't exaggerating about the shop; since she had last been in, Fran had hung several bright crazy quilts along the back wall.

"Thanks. I like to rearrange it every so often, especially in the middle of winter, to freshen it up a bit." Fran put her coffee on the counter and slipped off her coat. "Let me take your coat."

Maggie removed hers and handed it to Fran, who went into the back room with them. While waiting for Fran, Maggie took a sip of coffee and opened the bag of cookies. They might as well sample a couple. Next she sent Mackenzie a text to check in, relieved to get a message back immediately: *Everything's fine. Snickers says hurry home.*

Fran hurried out of the back room carrying the shiny chest, which she placed on the worktable. "After we have our coffee,

I'll put out the blocks and go over what needs to be done. I don't want to risk spilling on the blocks."

Feeling more relaxed after hearing Mackenzie was okay, Maggie enjoyed chatting with Fran while drinking her coffee and munching on a molasses cookie. She drained the last of her coffee. "I'm excited to hear what you're going to do with the blocks."

Fran tossed her own cup into the waste can. "Let's get to it then." Beckoning to Maggie, she headed over to the worktable. "Most of them just need light cleaning, fortunately, and maybe a little stitching." She opened the box lid, careful not to let it swing back on the hinges. "They're in surprisingly good—" Fran broke off with a gasp, one hand flying to her mouth.

"What's wrong?" Maggie peered into the box.

It was empty. The blocks were gone.

14

Maggie gripped the edge of the table, not believing the evidence of her eyes. "Fran, where are the quilt blocks?"

"I don't know." Fran put both hands to her cheeks. "They were there the other day . . . I was looking at them when I made a list of what needed to be done." She dashed to the counter and retrieved a folder, laid it on the table, and flipped it open. "See?"

Maggie perused the list, which detailed the picture on each block, the signature on the back, and what needed to be done. "I believe you." Her mind was spinning with the theft. "You're sure you didn't misplace them?"

"I could never be so careless with something so precious," Fran told her.

"Sorry. I had to ask." Maggie hurried for her phone. "I'm calling Robert Linton."

When Officer Linton arrived, he didn't appear to be impressed by the crime. "So someone took a bunch of old quilt blocks?" He stood with pen poised over his pad. "What's their estimated value?"

Maggie threw up her hands. "I have no idea. They're antique and irreplaceable. But they're probably more sentimental than anything." She turned to her friend. "What do you think, Fran?"

"Several hundred dollars, maybe a thousand. If the quilt had been assembled or someone famous had signed the blocks, they would be worth more. Modern quilts commonly sell for around a thousand, so I imagine one that's over a hundred years old would actually be even more valuable."

Maggie was shocked by the answer, and even Robert's eyebrows rose. "A thousand dollars—that's significant," the officer said. "But I can't see someone swiping them for a quick sale, like they do with electronics." He peered around the shop. "Anything else missing?"

"Not that I've noticed," Fran said. "I lock the shop whenever I'm not here. Even when I just go across the street for coffee."

"That's right," Maggie added. "I watched her unlock the door when we came in from The Bean just a little while ago."

Robert tucked his notebook into a pocket. "Let me take a look at the back door."

Maggie and Fran trailed along to the rear storage room, where Robert examined both sides of the back door. "See these scratches?" He pointed to barely visible marks around the lock. "Somebody picked this." He turned the doorknob back and forth. "You really should get a deadbolt. It's harder to tamper with those."

Fran nodded. "I'll call a locksmith today. I'm so sorry, Maggie."

"It's not your fault, Fran," Maggie assured her, but inside she was panicking. The blocks had been a key part of the historical society's plan to get stewardship of the lighthouse.

How would they save it now?

. . . .

"So the quilt blocks are missing?" Liz frowned in confusion. "But who would want them? Besides us, I mean."

Liz and Maggie were in the church office, getting ready to go through old parish records. Usually they were stored in the cellar, but that was an uncomfortable place to sit for long periods. Maggie was relieved to find that Liz had brought them upstairs.

"I have no idea who took them or why. They have some monetary value, but they're not exactly a typical snatch-and-grab item. Most people wouldn't know what they were worth, so the thief wouldn't be able to get much for them. I didn't know their value until Fran was telling Robert."

Liz swiveled back and forth in her chair, one hand on her chin. "Hmm. Who knew about them? Maybe we can narrow it down that way."

"Everyone who reads the paper, unfortunately. Adrian's article mentioned that Fran was going to restore the blocks. There was even a picture of the chest in the article, so where they were stored wasn't a mystery."

"Well, I hope they show up." Liz gestured at the ledgers awaiting their attention. "Should we still continue with our research? Without the blocks, the genealogy project is basically a bust."

Maggie's heart sank. Liz was right. In the back of her mind she had been hoping that learning about the other quiltmakers would reveal something about her own ancestor. "I suppose we could shelve it until they show up. And I'm praying they do. But we still have Mackenzie's quest. Let's see if we can find anything about Sarah Anne Stewart."

"I'm game if you are. How do you think we should proceed?"

Maggie thought for a moment. "We don't know for certain whether Stewart was Sarah Anne's married or maiden name. So let's go back a few decades from 1898, to 1870 or so, and look for any Stewarts."

"We're in luck. I brought up every ledger since 1850." She reached for the office radio. "How about a little classical music while we peruse?"

Strains of violins and organ music created a nice atmosphere while they searched through the ancient, dusty books, pausing now and then to sip some tea or stand up and stretch. In such a small parish, baptism, marriage, and funeral records were all listed in one book. The legibility of the handwriting varied by recorder and by the type of ink used.

"Okay," Maggie said. "I'm in 1898 and I haven't found any

marriage for Sarah Anne so far. And you found her baptism, so Stewart was definitely her birth name."

Liz lifted a finger. "Hold on. I think I've found her marriage. June 16, 1900. Sarah Anne Stewart married Harold Winston Carter. Both of Somerset Harbor."

"Harold Carter? As in Harry Carter?" Daisy's husband was descended from a long line of Somerset Harbor fishermen.

"We'll have to check to see if they're from the same family. But I bet they are."

Maggie felt a rush of excitement. "This is great. We've established a link between a stitcher and another member of the historical society. So far, we have Ina, Deborah, and Daisy. And me, I think, since Julia had the blocks."

"Unfortunately, this means Sarah Anne Carter isn't Mackenzie's great-great-grandmother," Liz pointed out.

"True." Maggie's spirits sank slightly. "But we still have Sarah Jane Mackenzie to check out." She crossed her fingers, hoping Mackenzie wouldn't end up disappointed.

. . . .

At Maggie's insistence, Mackenzie had spent the night at the manor again. The next morning, Maggie phoned Ruby's house and spoke to the day nurse, who said Ruby would welcome visitors. After breakfast, they bundled up for the journey over to see her.

Mackenzie's fingers fumbled as she zipped her coat. "I'm so excited. Do you think Sarah Jane is my great-great-grandmother?"

Maggie wound a scarf around her neck. "I hope so. She left Somerset Harbor after the quilt blocks were stitched, so it's possible." She picked up her tote bag. "Ready?"

"By the way, did you hear anything strange last night?" Mackenzie bent to tie her boot.

"No. Did you?" Maggie's pulse began to race. Had the mysterious tapper returned? But Mackenzie had slept upstairs. If anyone should have been disturbed, it was her, since her bedroom was on the first floor.

"Not really. But Snickers bolted out of the bedroom in the middle of the night and ran downstairs. When I came down to see if he was hungry or something, I found him sitting here in the hall, right in front of the door." She pointed to the spot.

"Did you hear anything?"

"No, not a peep. After a few minutes, I told Snickers my feet were cold, so I went back up to bed. He followed after a bit."

"Hmm. Maybe it was an animal sniffing around outside."

Maggie pulled open the front door and as it swung inward, Mackenzie gasped. "What's that?"

Maggie followed her gaze to what was attached to the door. Another note. Without thinking, she ripped it down, grateful a moment later that she had worn gloves. It was an old, sepia-toned photograph of a seated woman from the waist up. Crude Xs were inked in red across her eyes, and hand-lettering along the bottom read, *Quit butting into things that don't concern you.*

"What do they mean?" Mackenzie's wide eyes were filled with fear. "What things?"

"I don't know," Maggie said grimly, "but I'm calling the police." She thought she should put Officer Linton on speed dial.

Robert happened to be out on patrol nearby, so it was only a matter of minutes before he pulled into the manor's drive.

"Thanks for coming over, Robert," Maggie said when she answered the door.

"Anytime you need me, I'm here for you." He touched the brim of his hat in a salute. "What's up?" His eyes darted over to Mackenzie. "Feeling better, Miss Floyd?"

"I am, thank you, officer." Mackenzie attempted a smile,

but ever since the threat had been discovered, she had been uncharacteristically quiet.

Maggie showed Robert the defaced photograph lying on the hallway console table. "This was attached to the front door sometime during the night. Mackenzie says Snickers acted like he had heard something last night, and we found the note when we opened the door this morning."

"Tell me what happened last night, Miss Floyd." The efficient Robert already had his pad and pen ready. After Mackenzie took him through the events, he asked, "So do you have any idea what the threat refers to?"

"I really don't," Maggie said. "The blocks are missing, so it can't be because of them. All we're doing is researching family history anyway. Yesterday we found out that one stitcher is probably related to Harry Carter's family."

"That doesn't sound like it should upset anyone," Robert said. "Aunt Ina told me that my great-grandmother made a square. I thought that was interesting."

"I hope no one's upset because we're going to visit Ruby Adams," Mackenzie said. "What if someone doesn't want us to?"

"What's this about Ruby Adams?" Robert asked.

Maggie explained that the elderly woman was also related to one maker of a quilt block, and they were going to visit her that morning. Mackenzie took up the story, explaining that she was looking for possible relatives in Somerset Harbor.

"I remember reading that in the *Herald*. Good luck. I doubt anyone would be upset by you visiting Ms. Adams either. Who even knows you're going, besides the two of you?" Robert turned back to the note. "I'll take that to the station. Call me if anything else happens, okay? We'll get to the bottom of this."

All the way out to Ruby's house, Mackenzie's phone dinged incessantly. "Sorry," she said after what seemed like the twentieth time. "I seem to be super popular today." With a grin, she typed away.

"No problem," Maggie said. "I'm still not used to how young people always communicate by text. It's the fastest way to get an answer out of my daughter."

"Yeah, that's true." A minute later, the phone dinged again, and Mackenzie said, "Aw, he's so sweet."

"Who?" Maggie ventured, hoping she wouldn't hear that Cody Becker was communicating with Mackenzie.

"Tyler. He just asked me to be his date to the Valentine's Day dinner at the Oceanview."

"I'm going to that too." Maggie realized she *still* hadn't spoken to James. Mackenzie squealed. "Really? Who's your date?"

"James Bennett."

"The town alderman? He's handsome. And really nice. He gives us big tips at The Bean."

"James *is* nice."

"What are you wearing?"

"You know, I haven't even thought about it," Maggie said, startled to realize it was the truth.

"I have the perfect thing picked out already—a little red dress. With matching shoes."

Noticing the stars in the young woman's eyes, Maggie's stomach clenched. She had to say something. "Um, Mackenzie. How's it going with Tyler?"

Mackenzie's eyes sharpened. *Uh-oh.* She hadn't been fooled by Maggie's casual tone. "You think he's too old for me."

Maggie seized that avenue with relief. It was much easier than bringing up Jed's warning or Fran's bad experience with Tyler. "Maybe a little. He is very handsome, though."

"You sound just like my mom." Mackenzie crossed her arms across her chest.

"Isn't that a good thing?" Maggie asked gently.

Mackenzie cocked her head and considered. "Yeah, it is, actually. Don't worry, I'm not rushing into anything. It's just a dinner."

"Good. Neither am I. But it will be fun to dress up. If I can figure out what to wear."

At Ruby's house, they found that the driveway was plowed and a pretty blue SUV sat near the back door. *It must be the nurse's car.* "Here we are."

The nurse, a pleasant-looking middle-aged woman, answered the door. "Maggie and Mackenzie, right? Come on in. Ruby's been looking forward to your visit."

They stamped the snow off their boots on the step and went inside the warm kitchen, which had something savory bubbling on the stove.

"Let me take your coats," the nurse said. "I'm Susan, by the way."

"Nice to meet you," Maggie said, slipping off her boots.

"It smells good in here," Mackenzie said, sniffing appreciatively.

"Doesn't it, though?" Susan agreed. "A nice lady from the church stopped by with a pot of homemade chicken dumpling soup."

"How nice." Maggie was glad Ruby was being cared for properly. She made a resolution to visit on a regular basis. It must be really hard to be elderly and alone way out here in the country.

Susan showed them into the living room, where Ruby was nestled in a recliner with an afghan across her lap and an open book in her hands. Although still pale, her curly gray hair was neatly brushed, and she wore an attractive raspberry velour robe.

The older woman looked up from her book and smiled. "Maggie. Thanks for coming over." She slid a bookmark into the volume—a mystery novel, judging by the title—and set it aside. "And you must be Mackenzie. I hear your folks came from Somerset Harbor."

Mackenzie perched on the sofa beside Maggie. "I think so.

That's what my mom told me." She reached for her knapsack and unzipped the front pocket. "All I have is this picture of my great-great-grandparents." She pulled out the photograph and handed it to Ruby.

Ruby studied the photograph. "Handsome couple." She turned it over. "Hmm. Sarah and John, 1898."

"Is that your great-aunt?" Maggie asked eagerly.

Mackenzie grabbed Maggie's hand anxiously while Ruby studied the picture. When Ruby said, "No, I don't think so," Mackenzie gave a soft groan of disappointment.

Ruby pointed at the box of papers Maggie had brought down from the second floor. "I saw a photograph in there. Let's compare to be sure."

Mackenzie made another sound, this one a yelp of excitement. She jumped up, grabbed the box, and set it beside Ruby's chair.

Ruby gaped at the jumble of papers in the box. "What happened in here?"

Maggie explained how she had found the box tipped over, with its contents strewn on the carpet. "I'm sorry I didn't organize anything. I wanted to get them off the floor, and I didn't know how you had them."

An odd expression flitted across Ruby's face and she frowned. Then her face paled.

"What's wrong, Ruby?" Maggie asked.

"Remember the day I went to the hospital? I thought I heard someone in here. But when I called out, no one answered."

Alarm jolted Maggie. It appeared someone had entered Ruby's house without permission while she lay sick in bed and rummaged through her belongings. But who? And was anything else missing?

"Should we look around and make sure everything is here?" Mackenzie suggested.

"Just to set your mind at ease," Maggie added, not wanting the frail woman to relapse due to distress and shock over even the possibility of being robbed.

"All right. There are only a few things worth much, besides my antique furniture. And if that was gone, I'd have known right away." She listed china, paintings, and decorative items for Maggie and Mackenzie to check.

A short while later, Maggie returned to the living room, followed by Mackenzie. "Everything appears to be here."

"That's good," Ruby said. She gestured at the box of papers. "While you were doing that, I looked through the box. There's only one thing missing as far as I can tell—the picture of my great-aunt."

Mackenzie gave a soft wail of dismay. "Oh no!"

Stumped, Maggie sank down on the sofa. "But who would want that photo?"

Ruby shook her head. "I have no idea. I hadn't even thought about her for years until you came over. And I'm her only living relative."

"That we know of," Mackenzie said.

"That we know of," Ruby echoed. "Unless—" She snapped her fingers. "There were some other young women in the photograph. Maybe the thief was interested in one of them."

"Do you know who the others were?" Maggie thought about the photograph of the quilting group that had gone missing from the lighthouse.

To her disappointment, Ruby shook her head. "No, it just said *My friends and me.* I remember that much."

"Do you want us to call the police?" Maggie groaned inwardly at the idea of calling Officer Linton twice in one day. At this rate, the police department might as well assign him to her full time.

Ruby sniffed. "For an old photo? Why bother? It's a shame, that's all."

Susan appeared in the doorway. "Soup's on, if you're ready for lunch, Ruby."

"Would you two like to stay?" Ruby asked, her eyes hopeful.

"There's plenty," added the helpful Susan.

"Are you hungry?" Maggie asked Mackenzie, who nodded enthusiastically. Maggie grinned in the face of a young person's bottomless appetite. "Thanks, we'd love to stay for lunch." She rose from the couch. "Let me help."

They ate at tray tables in the living room, and as they enjoyed the savory soup with its broad noodles and assorted veggies, Maggie felt herself relaxing. The atmosphere in the room perceptively lightened, and Mackenzie and Ruby fell into a conversation ranging from Ruby's childhood in Somerset Harbor to Mackenzie's life in Boston to art.

"What wonderful work," Ruby said when Mackenzie displayed her sketchbook. "You're really talented."

Mackenzie beamed, her cheeks flushing with pleasure. "Thanks. As an artist, you're never sure if what you've done is good or garbage."

"Good—definitely good," Ruby said. "I can't draw a straight line myself." She closed the book and handed it back to Mackenzie.

"Would you let me draw you?" Mackenzie asked shyly as she tucked the book back into her pack.

"Me? I'm no beauty."

"Sure you are. Your face has tons of character."

Peals of surprised laughter broke from Ruby. "Mackenzie Floyd, you're a tonic. I haven't had such a nice time in weeks."

Maggie took in the excited faces of the elderly woman and the young artist. A solid rapport had been ignited during this visit and she was glad. Even if they weren't related, she had the feeling the two were becoming fast friends. *Each could certainly use a friend.* Maybe something good would come out of the mysteries surrounding the quilt blocks after all.

A little later, as she and Mackenzie made their goodbyes and trudged out to the car through thick-falling snowflakes, the sound of speeding tires on wet pavement caught her ear. She turned toward the road to see who was driving so carelessly in the snow.

The white pickup slowed as it passed the driveway, the rear end slewing back and forth. Then the driver gunned the motor and raced away.

"Someone broke into Ruby's house and stole an old photograph?" June's face showed shock and disbelief as Maggie told her the story the next morning. She pushed aside the store inventory sheets and focused on Maggie, cupping her chin in her hand. "That is one of the strangest things I've ever heard."

"I agree. Someone did the same thing out at the lighthouse." Maggie forced herself to sound brave. "And there's the matter of the threatening notes I've been getting."

June sat bolt upright, her mouth dropping open. "Threatening notes! I hope you called the police."

"Of course. I think Robert Linton has gotten to the point where he knows his calls are from me and doesn't even have to check the caller ID. He's concerned about the threats but he didn't seem to care much that the quilt blocks were stolen."

June patted her chest. "I care. I think it's awful." Her eyes narrowed. "All these weird events must have something to do with those blocks. They all started happening after you found them, right?"

"Well, right after the newspaper article about them. And I still don't understand why someone seems to be targeting Mackenzie." The doctor had cleared Mackenzie to go back to work, and the young woman had insisted on going home, promising Maggie that she would be safe and avoid being alone as much as possible.

The bells attached to the shop door jingled and they looked over to see James Bennett step inside, bundled in a parka, hat, and gloves.

"Good morning, ladies." James nodded as he stamped snow off his boots. "How are you today?"

They chorused greetings, then June asked, "Are you here to look at the veneer on the oak hutch?"

"I'll do that later today. Maggie, I stopped by to see if you'd like to drive out to the lighthouse with me. I'm working on the inspection for the society." He gave her a charming, crooked smile. "I figured you've already been there once, so you can show me around."

"You do building inspections too? Is there anything you can't do?" Maggie asked, to stall while she tried to figure out an answer. At the thought of driving alone with James out to the secluded lighthouse, she squirmed inwardly, torn between a bold yes and the urge to run and hide. There would be no avoiding talking about the Valentine's Day dinner if she went. On the other hand, the longer she waited, the more difficult it was becoming to broach the topic.

James grinned. "I've found that in a small town, it's useful to be multitalented. I got my license a few years ago, but I only do inspections on an as-needed basis. Can you come?"

June elbowed Maggie. "Of course she'd like to go."

"I hate to leave you in the middle of inventory," Maggie said.

June gathered the papers and stacked them neatly. "That can wait. It's a nice day and fairly warm. I'll probably be busy with customers soon. Tomorrow's dipping into the single digits, though, right, James?"

"That's right. It will be near zero tonight. This is the last good day for a week."

"If you're sure, June . . ." At her friend's nod, Maggie grinned at James. "Then I'm all yours." When she heard her own words, her cheeks burned. Ducking her head to hide her flaming face, she hurried to the coat rack. Hopefully the winter air would cool her off.

With James behind the wheel of his classic black Mercedes,

they drove through town and out into the countryside. James was silent and Maggie gazed out at the passing houses and scenery, content to be a passenger for once.

When a black truck came toward them, James raised a hand to wave at the driver. As the other vehicle passed, Maggie recognized Jed Parker. "You know Jed?"

"Who doesn't? He's one of the characters that make Somerset Harbor so interesting."

Maggie had to agree with that. "I was out at his store the other day, and when his neighbor had an emergency, he went racing over there."

"That's Jed all right. A good man to have around." Suddenly, James shook his head with a chuckle.

"What?" Maggie asked.

"I was just remembering a story he told me. You met his old hound, Bessie?" Maggie nodded. "There was a black bear that was coming around his yard every night to get into the trash cans."

"You get bears too?" Maggie broke in. "They finally passed a law in Vermont so people would stop feeding them." A thought struck her. "This isn't the stuffed bear that's upstairs in his store?"

"No way. Jed wouldn't shoot anything. Or stuff it."

"That's a relief. Go on."

"Every night when the bear would come around, Bessie would run after it, barking. The bear would climb a certain tree and stay up there until Jed called Bessie off. It got to be quite a ritual—went on for weeks. Well, one night Bessie tore off across the yard to the tree and stood there barking. But the bear wasn't up there yet. Suddenly the bear came trotting across the yard, climbed over the dog, and scooted up the tree."

Maggie burst out laughing. "It's like the bear and Bessie were playing a game."

"Exactly. You would have thought the bear would run the other way, not climb over the dog to get into position."

The shared merriment broke the ice and Maggie suddenly felt entirely at ease with James for the first time in days. She would focus on enjoying his company, she decided, and if there was a good moment to discuss the dinner, she would. *No more stressing out over it.*

Her cell phone rang in her handbag and she debated whether or not to answer. "Go ahead," James said. "It might be business." He winked. "When you work for yourself, it's important to be available."

Maggie dug out the phone and saw the Carriage House Antiques number on the screen. "You're right, it is business." She answered. "Hi, June. What's up?"

"You'll never guess who wants us to look at some furniture to buy."

"Who?"

"Tyler Monroe."

Maggie gave an involuntary gasp. "Tyler Monroe?" James frowned at the name. "He wants us to buy furniture from the Monroe Mansion? He said something about that the other day, but I didn't think he'd actually call." She had to admit, she was extremely interested in getting inside that house. In addition to being the home of a missing heiress, it was gorgeous in its own right.

"That's what he said. Listen, Maggie, no pressure, but he wanted us out there today. You two are going by there. Do you think . . ."

Maggie got it. Turning to her companion, she asked, "James, do you mind if we stop by Monroe Mansion on the way back? Tyler wants to sell some furniture."

"Fine with me. I've always wanted to get inside that place

myself." He grinned. "And you never know, I might pick up some restoration work."

"We'll be there in a couple of hours, June. Can you let him know? Thanks."

Today no one was out at the lighthouse. After James looked around outside, he produced a key and they went inside. While he surveyed the downstairs and made notes on a clipboard, Maggie went to the office and scanned the photos. Adrian had been right—the one of the quilting group was missing. In fact, there hadn't even been an attempt to hide that fact by rearranging the other pictures. The blank spot stared at her like an accusing eye.

"This place is certainly quaint." James appeared in the doorway, then wandered over to look at the old monitoring equipment. "Like a time capsule."

"Ina said it hadn't changed since she was here as a teenager." Maggie showed James the faded photograph of Ina and the lighthouse family. "See?"

James chuckled at the sight of a much younger Ina. "She doesn't look much different. And obviously her personality hasn't changed. Still spunky as ever."

Maggie pointed at the blank spot. "And there used to be a picture of Sarah Monroe right there."

"Really? I've never seen a picture of her. Did you take it for the society?"

Maggie gave a soft groan of frustration. "No. It's missing." She recited the series of mysterious events that had been plaguing her and the quilt blocks project.

James frowned, creating a deep crease between his brows. "Why didn't you tell me all this before?"

His tone was sharp and Maggie bristled. "I didn't realize I had to report to you." She turned and stalked away from him. If he got bossy and demanding just because she'd agreed to one date, well, he could forget any such future events. Richard had never been like that, ever. At least, not without good reason.

"Maggie, wait. I didn't mean that the way it sounded."

She whirled around. "I hope not." Jutting her chin out, she said, "I was confiding in you as a friend, not my keeper."

He took a step toward her. "I'm sorry." Now his frown conveyed remorse. "I'm concerned about you, that's all. I don't like these threats."

Maggie snorted. "It's not exactly a picnic for me either."

He came closer. "That's not what I mean. I care about you, Maggie. Isn't it obvious?" His blue-gray eyes were lit with a gentle fire.

Maggie took a step back involuntarily. She was starting to care about him too, and it confused her. Her muscles tensed and her pulse began to race. Putting off the discussion about the Valentine's Day dinner any longer would be hurtful and rude. Mustering her courage, she blurted, "James, I'm not sure about going to the Oceanview with you." There—it was out.

Confusion and hurt clouded his eyes. "What do you mean?"

"I mean . . ." What did she mean? Emily's words popped into her head. *Too much too soon.* "Well, I'm sure it's a wonderful event, but don't you think it's a little much . . . so soon?"

A series of expressions flickered over his face—more confusion, thoughtfulness, then comprehension. "Oh, I get it. Going to a grand event on Valentine's Day is rather a statement, isn't it? I didn't even think of that. The event has amazing food for a good cause, and I enjoy spending time with you. That's about as far as my thought process went. I'm sorry."

Maggie's shoulders slumped in relief. He hadn't meant the date as a declaration of true undying love or anything so dramatic after all. "In that case, I'd still love to go." She gave him a warm smile. "Thanks for asking me."

"Now that that's cleared up, let's get on with the tour." He studied the room. "How do we get up in the tower?"

In the observation room, James pulled a thermos and two cups from his rucksack, and they enjoyed a cup of coffee while gazing at the view. Today was sparkling clear again, and Maggie savored the view of waves crashing against the rugged shore.

"I'd hate to be on the water today," Maggie commented. "I wonder if Harry Carter went out."

"It probably depends on how long his honey-do list is at present," James said with a grin. "But you can bet he probably went out if he could. Those lobstermen are a lot hardier than I am."

"Oh, speaking of Harry, we found one of our Sarahs. I think she's related to Harry." She told James about Sarah's marriage to Harold Winston Carter.

"I think Winston is Harry's middle name, so I think you've got a winner. He's probably named after that exact ancestor."

"We'll have to stop by The Bean and tell Daisy about it later." Maggie mulled over the quilt blocks mystery. "Did I tell you what my Aunt Evelyn wrote about the blocks? *Sometimes being a friend means keeping a secret.*"

"Intriguing," James said. "I wonder what the secret is that someone doesn't want you to uncover."

"Me too. I can't imagine why a hundred-year-old mystery is so important that someone would skulk around and steal to stop us investigating."

"Be careful, okay?" At Maggie's suspicious glare, James added hastily, "I mean that in a friendly way, not a bossy one." He drained his cup. "Let's go to Tyler's. I think I have all I need here."

As they approached Monroe Mansion, which was set behind a rusty black-iron fence with pointed spikes, Maggie reflected that the mansard roof style resembled something on the cover of a gothic novel. James drove around the semicircular drive and parked in front of the granite steps. From this close vantage point, she clearly saw peeling paint, loose shutter slats, and a missing shingle or two. The place had the air of a tattered but proud beauty, the leaning barn in the rear like a sagging bustle on her dress.

The porch boards were creaky too and covered in chipped gray paint. "Lots of opportunity to do restoration here," she whispered to James after he pulled the hanging doorbell rope.

"I'd love a big project like this," he whispered back. "They don't build houses like this anymore." He straightened as the front door opened to reveal Tyler Monroe.

Although at home and presumably relaxing, the man still wore dress pants, shirt, and tie, although the last was loose at least, Maggie was glad to see. *Is he ever casual?*

"Thanks for coming over so promptly." Tyler's eyes went to James. "You part of the antiques business now, James?" He didn't appear pleased to have the additional visitor.

"We happened to be on an errand together," Maggie said. "James isn't officially part of the business, but he does do our furniture restoration."

"I can wait in the car if you'd prefer," James offered.

Tyler stepped back. "That won't be necessary. Actually, I have a piece that needs fixing. Maybe you can take a look, since you're here."

"Be happy to," James said.

The hallway was classic late Victorian, with black and white tile blocks on the floor and a curved, soaring staircase to the second floor. The paneling appeared to be ornately carved walnut, as were the balusters and handrail. But as Maggie peered more closely, she saw a slight shabbiness that spoke of long neglect.

Through double doors to the left and right, she glimpsed a crowded, magnificently furnished parlor and dining room.

Swagged velvet drapes and a plethora of fussy knickknacks and ornaments also indicated the last era in which the rooms had been decorated.

"Have you decided which things you're selling?" Maggie had learned that some customers already knew what they wanted to get rid of, while others preferred to get appraisals and then make a decision.

Tyler seemed overwhelmed. "There's just so much stuff." He indicated the parlor and the dining room. "Down here I'd like to have you give me appraisals, since I might keep the more valuable things. But I do know I want to clean out the bedrooms upstairs. The beds are too small and the mattresses are terrible."

Maggie headed for the stairs, carrying her tote, which contained a notebook and pen and a digital camera. "I'll start up there, then."

"The piece I want you to look at is in the dining room," Tyler said to James, and the two men disappeared in that direction.

The staircase was adorned by a Persian rug runner, another item that spoke to the care and expense once lavished on the home. The upstairs hall was wide, with five open doors leading off it. Four appeared to be bedrooms, and the one in the back was a bathroom, complete with a claw-foot tub and a commode with a wooden seat.

Starting in the front, Maggie took pictures of the four-poster beds and matching bureaus and dressers. Tyler had been right; these were all full-size, and most people now preferred queen or larger. She hoped she could sell the furniture to antique buffs who cared more about authenticity than comfort.

The bedroom in the rear had a feminine air, with wisteria wallpaper and pale lavender draperies and bedding. Unlike the other rooms, this one gave the impression of having gone untouched for decades. Dust lay thick on the carved inlaid furniture. A Bible, a silver hairbrush, and a bowl of hairpins sat by the bedside and on the dressing table. A small bookcase held a number of faded leather-bound volumes.

A shiver ran down Maggie's spine. This was Sarah Monroe's bedroom; she just knew it. And by the looks of things, it had remained untouched since her mysterious disappearance. She stepped inside, feeling almost like she was entering a shrine.

A cross-stitch sampler with the alphabet and letters on the wall confirmed her theory. The slightly crooked stitching of a young Sarah reported, *Sarah Monroe, age 10, did this work in the year of our Lord 1886.*

She wondered if Tyler would sell her Sarah's personal items. They would make a nice addition to the scarf they already had at the museum. A battered portfolio lying on top of the bookcase caught her eye. Curious, she opened the cover and discovered that Sarah Monroe had been an artist, and quite an accomplished one, judging by the sketches of the lighthouse, Old Faith Chapel, and the Sedgwick mansion.

There was something familiar about the scenes, and after a moment it struck her: Sarah Monroe had designed the quilt blocks. She was looking at the original designs in this sketchbook.

Maggie took a few snaps of the sketches, her pulse humming with excitement. This piece of information would add a great deal to their exhibit—if they found the blocks. She took photos of the furniture and made notes, then scurried downstairs, wondering how to raise the issue with Tyler. She would never sell her aunt's personal items; maybe he would feel the same about Sarah's. She would have to tread gently.

In the dining room, she found the two men examining a breakfront hutch, a gorgeous specimen with three glass bays.

"You think you can fix that?" Tyler asked. "If so, I definitely want to get rid of that thing. Too old-fashioned and heavy."

"If I can find a piece of similar wood." James threw a glance back over his shoulder and spotted her. "Maggie, come take a look at this."

She crossed the room, curious to see what they were so engrossed in. When she reached his side, James stepped back and pointed to a circular hole in the middle of the cabinet at the level of his forehead. He put his finger in the opening.

"I believe that is a bullet hole."

16

Maggie gasped. "A bullet hole? How did it get there?"

"A gun, obviously," Tyler said flippantly, crossing his arms. "When, who, or why, I have no idea."

"Is there any way to tell?"

"Someone tried to cover it up, we know that much." James showed Maggie some crumbled wood putty he'd placed on a napkin on the dining room table. "But as the wood aged and got darker, the putty became more obvious."

"It stuck out like a sore thumb," Tyler agreed. "Every time I came in here, my eyes were drawn right to it."

"We may know more once I dig the bullet out," James said. He went to the side of the cabinet and peered around the edge, shifting the cabinet slightly with a grunt. "Given how heavy this piece is, I doubt it's been moved since the incident happened. I wonder if the bullet went all the way through the cabinet and into the wall."

"That must be thick wood if it didn't," Maggie noted.

"They don't make furniture like this anymore, out of solid boards. Want to help me, Tyler?" With grunts the two men shifted the cabinet far enough out to reveal that the bullet was indeed still inside it, not in the wall behind it. The trio regarded the back of the hutch in silence, Maggie's mind thrumming with theories. Had Sarah Monroe been shot? Or was the incident of more recent vintage?

"How was the upstairs?" Tyler asked Maggie.

She pulled out her notebook. "Great. I'll have to go over my notes with June, but I think we'll buy all the furniture." Asking him about the sketchbook was on the tip of her tongue, but she lost her courage in the face of his aloof, almost forbidding expression.

"You didn't go in the rear bedroom, did you, the one with the purple wallpaper?"

Uh-oh. "Actually, the door was open, so I did."

"You didn't mention that one was off-limits," James said mildly. "But no problem, right, Maggie?"

"That's right, no problem. Things from there are off the list." Maggie crossed out the list of Sarah's furniture. *Thank goodness I didn't ask about Sarah's personal belongings.*

"I can send a truck for the cabinet," James said, "unless you want to bring it over to the shop yourself. I'll be working on it at Carriage House Antiques."

Tyler's eyes narrowed. "In my BMW? I don't think so."

James put both hands up. "Sorry. Just asking. Some customers prefer to handle their own items."

"I'll call you later with prices for the bedroom furniture," Maggie said. "If we come to an agreement regarding price, we'll get someone to pick it up." Maybe she could hire Bobby Linton and his friend Jarrod Rodgers, as she had in the past. Bobby was Robert and Nora Linton's son, and he and Jarrod were her go-to moving crew. She'd never met two more careful and hardworking high school seniors.

They finished making their arrangements, and then Maggie and James made good their escape. On the front porch again, they exchanged looks with raised eyebrows.

"Wow," she said. "He's a tough one."

"That's for sure." James took her arm as they made their way down the steps and onto the path. "But it looks like you'll be able to buy some good inventory from him."

Maggie and James stopped in at The Busy Bean for lunch. Mackenzie bustled up to take their order. "What can I get you?

Special today is bean-and-bacon soup with a side of cheddar scones. The scones are little so you get two."

Maggie and James exchanged nods. "Two specials, please," James said.

"And two coffees," Maggie added. She was still chilled from their time at the lighthouse and was looking forward to some hot food and drink.

"Right away," Mackenzie said cheerfully. "We have a great Ethiopian roast today. Want that?"

"Sure," James said. "I gather you're feeling better, Mackenzie."

"Thanks, Mr. Bennett." Her eyes sparkled so that it was hard to believe she had been in the hospital just days before. "I couldn't wait to get back to work. Although recuperating at Maggie's house was fantastic."

"I bet. Maggie's a great hostess."

Maggie blushed and changed the subject. "Mackenzie, is Daisy here? If she is, I'd like to talk to her." She wanted to share the news about Sarah Anne Stewart.

Mackenzie jerked her thumb toward the kitchen. "She's in the back. I'll tell her you're here."

After the young waitress hurried off, James said, "I'm looking forward to investigating that bullet hole. I must say, fixing that type of damage will be a first for me."

"I'll give Bobby Linton a call. Maybe he can pick it up after school." Maggie leaned back so Mackenzie could deliver their coffee mugs before whirling away again. "Of course, he's often busy with sports and other activities, so it may be a day or two."

"I know someone else—Jed Parker. He mostly uses his truck for his own merchandise, but he'll do general delivery for a fee. I can call him if you'd like, see if he can do it today."

"That would be great. Thanks."

While James spoke to Jed on the phone—which sounded like a lively discussion—Daisy came out of the kitchen carrying their plates. She set them down and wiped her hands on her apron.

"Enjoy. That's an old family recipe from Harry's mother," she said.

What a perfect segue. "Guess what Liz and I discovered in the church archives?" Maggie asked as she took a sip of the hearty soup. "Wow."

"Glad you like it." Daisy cocked her head. "Now spill your news before I have to shake it out of you."

Maggie set her spoon down. "We found Sarah Anne Stewart. It turns out she married a Harold Winston Carter, and we thought that might be one of Harry's ancestors."

"I bet it is. If Harry's family was fancy enough to use Roman numerals, he'd be Harold Winston IV."

"That's another Sarah down, then." Maggie lowered her voice. "I also found out today that Sarah Monroe designed those quilt blocks."

Daisy's eyes widened. "Really? How'd you do that?"

Maggie explained her trip to Tyler's house and how she had snooped—innocently, of course—in Sarah's old bedroom.

Before Daisy could comment, James hung up. "We're all set. Jed will get the hutch today, and then he'll go back and get the bedroom furniture another day if Bobby can't go." He noticed Daisy standing there. "Sorry, didn't mean to interrupt."

"No, that's fine," Daisy said. "I've got to get back to the kitchen anyway. Maggie, we'll talk more at the historical society meeting." With a wave, she headed across the room.

James added pepper and salt to his soup and took a spoonful. "Yum. Good pick." They ate in silence for a few minutes. Then James piped up. "Jed said something odd. He told me that Tyler does have a truck; in fact, he 'stole' it right out from under Jed's nose when it was for sale at one of the garages in town. So Tyler could have brought the hutch over."

Maggie considered this new information. "I can see why he might not want to, since that hutch is a heavy beast. I wonder why he lied about having a truck, though."

James shook his head. "If I had to stop and try to figure why folks do what they do, I'd never get anything else done."

Mackenzie circled back by the table, holding a coffeepot. "Top up?" Maggie nodded as did James, and Mackenzie filled their mugs. "Would either of you like dessert?"

"None for me—" Maggie broke off when she noticed Mackenzie staring toward The Busy Bean's front door, all the color drained from her face. She swiveled in her seat to look.

Cody Becker stood in the doorway, fists clenching as he swung his head back and forth, scanning the crowd. *Oh no.* Maggie had hoped the young man had left town after his disastrous visit to Somerset Harbor. Maybe he'd had to return for a court hearing about his drunk driving offense.

"I've got to go." Mackenzie fled.

Cody saw her dart toward the kitchen and followed, his long legs striding across the floor.

"James, you've got to stop him!" Maggie cried.

"Who?"

Maggie realized that James didn't know anything about Cody Becker; it hadn't occurred to her to tell him yet. She rose to her feet, pointing. "That's Mackenzie's ex-boyfriend. He's known to be violent."

Her word was good enough for James; he sprang from his chair and dashed to intercept Cody, who had reached the swinging kitchen door. The other patrons stopped their chatter to stare, guessing something was up.

James put out his arm and barred Cody from entering the

kitchen. They had a low-voiced but vehement debate. James put his arm around Cody's shoulders and began to lead him away from the kitchen. Maggie heaved a sigh and sank back into her chair, relieved that the situation was resolved.

Suddenly Cody wrenched away from James and delivered a powerful right hook to his face. Someone screamed. Maggie jumped up as James flung himself at Cody, trying to restrain his arms. They bumped into a table, sending a couple of coffee mugs crashing to the floor while the customers scrambled to get out of the way.

"I've called the police," one elderly man yelled out, waving his phone. "They're on their way."

Daisy and Jack, the cook, burst from the kitchen, and Jack threw himself into the fray. It took the combined efforts of James and Jack to get the belligerent young man under control. In the end, James sat on his chest, holding down his arms, and Jack pinned his legs.

Lights flashed outside the diner, and Robert Linton rushed in, followed by his sometimes-partner, Janeen Crosby. Maggie began to relax as they cuffed Cody, but she shuddered when she caught a glimpse of the young man's face.

His fierce expression could only mean one thing: *This isn't over.*

· · · · · · · · · · · · · · · · ·

"Are you sure you're up for this?" Maggie asked James. They were in the back room of Carriage House Antiques, examining the breakfront hutch Jed had dropped off earlier.

James, who sported a swollen cheek, nodded. Then he groaned. "I keep forgetting not to move my head too fast. That guy had quite a swing."

"Do you want another ice pack?" The emergency room doctor had recommended icing to reduce the swelling. "I can run over to the manor for some more."

"No, I'll ice it again later. Right now I want to dig out that bullet." James selected a craft knife and an awl from the assortment of tools on the workbench.

June walked into the room. "The last customer just left, so I put up the Closed sign. I didn't miss the bullet, did I?"

"No, you're just in time for the show." Maggie leaned against the bench. June joined her, and they watched as James carefully enlarged the hole, alternating the knife and the awl.

"I don't want to remove any more material than necessary," James explained. Once he was satisfied with the opening, he laid the tools aside and picked up a pair of needle-nose pliers. After a little effort and muttering, he extracted the hunk of metal, holding it aloft triumphantly. "It's a bullet all right. So now the question is, who was trying to kill whom in the Monroe Mansion, and did they eventually succeed?"

17

Maggie's first thought was that someone had shot at Sarah Monroe. But she bit back this theory and asked instead, "Is there any way to tell how old it is?"

James gently set the bullet on a piece of cloth. "You could get it analyzed to find out the caliber and a guestimate on the age. If it's a rare type, that might make it easier."

"Another mystery," June said. "Do you think Tyler did it himself?"

James folded his arms and considered the piece of furniture. "I don't think so, judging by the apparent age of the wood putty that was stuck in there. But if he did, there's no law against shooting your own belongings as long as no one got hurt."

"Besides why would he draw attention to it now?" Maggie asked. "Even if James does a nice repair—which he will—the value has been compromised."

"Maybe a bullet hole will add cachet," June suggested. "You never know with collectors."

If they did learn that bullet was related to the disappearance of Sarah Monroe and the news got out, it might stir public interest. With all the strange things that had started happening after the public became aware that there was any interest in the quilt blocks and the women who'd made them, Maggie wasn't sure she wanted the public's interest anymore.

James glanced at his watch. "Shoot. I better get going. I've got another appointment." He put his tools away in their box. "I'll be back tomorrow or the next day to start working on the hutch." Then he grinned at Maggie. "But I'll see you tomorrow night. Pick you up at six?"

Maggie's cheeks heated up under June's amused gaze. "That sounds fine. See you then."

After he left, Maggie turned to June. "I can't believe it. The dinner is tomorrow night and I don't have a thing to wear."

"Don't sweat it. The event is semiformal, which means an elegant blouse and a skirt or a dress. Men wear suit coats and ties."

"Can you help me, June? I really don't have a clue what to wear. Maybe you can help me put something together from my closet."

June's eyes lit up. "I'd love to."

The two women headed over to the mansion and into the massive closet off the master bath.

"Wow." June looked around at the racks and drawers, the shelves and shoe trees. "What a fantastic closet."

"I know." Maggie gestured at her clothing, which barely filled a third of the space. "I don't have to put away my seasonal wardrobes anymore. I can leave them out all year." She went to the rack that held her slim selection of fancy clothes, the things she'd worn to faculty parties or out to dinner with Richard. "Tell me what you think."

June leafed through the blouses and slacks, skirts and dresses, a thoughtful frown creasing her brow. Once in a while she pulled something out, considered it, and put it back.

As Maggie watched, butterflies began to flutter in her belly. It had been so long since she'd enjoyed a special occasion. "This dinner is really fun, June?" She heard both hope and doubt in her tone.

"Oh definitely. It's one of the highlights of the year. It really brightens up the dead of winter. They decorate the hotel beautifully, and the food is absolutely scrumptious. You won't find anything nicer in this area."

The butterflies flapped harder. "Now that James and I have talked about the Valentine's Day issue, I'm so glad he asked me. I'm really looking forward to it."

"You got that cleared up? Good. You'll love it. Kurt and I do." June finally pulled out two items, a creamy silk blouse and a pair of wide-legged black velvet pants. "I think you should wear these. They're both made with lovely material, and this blouse will bring out your skin and hair in the candlelight."

Maggie liked June's selection. Both pieces were comfortable and flattering. "What shoes should I wear?"

June browsed Maggie's selection and picked out a pair of black pumps. "Now you just need some jewelry and you're all set. Pearls if you have them."

"I do," Maggie said. "Earrings and necklace. That was easy. Maybe you can be my personal wardrobe consultant."

"Anytime." June strolled briskly out of the closet. "I'd better get home and start dinner if I'm going to make it to the historical society meeting tonight."

"Oh, I almost forgot about that. I'll see you there." Maggie walked June to the door and returned to the kitchen, where Snickers was waiting for his dinner. After feeding him, Maggie opened the refrigerator to peruse the contents. "What should I have for supper, Snickers?"

Her cell phone rang and she dashed to retrieve it from the hallway where she had left her bag. "Hi, Liz. What's up? Ready for the meeting tonight?"

"I am, but that's not why I'm calling." As always, her friend's voice was warm and soothing. "I'm down at the jail, and there's someone here who wants to see you."

"Liz, I'm sorry, but I'm lost." *Who in jail would want to see me?*

"Let me take a step back. You know David has a ministry with prisoners, right? He visits them and brings them Bibles. Usually he goes to the county prison, but Somerset Harbor occasionally keeps some inmates for a night or two. The police station has a couple of holding cells, remember?"

"Got it. And there is someone at the station who wants to talk to me?" Then her stomach slid down into her toes. "Don't tell me. Cody Becker."

"Yes, that's right. I know you've had some run-ins with him. Maggie, he's just a hurt and confused young man, not a hardened criminal. Anyway, he insists that he wants to apologize to you in person for the trouble he's caused."

"Oh, Liz, are you sure that's a good idea? This afternoon he popped James right in the face."

"You'll be safe, Maggie, I promise. He's in his cell, and there'll be an officer right there. David thinks it might help him. He's going to get Cody into therapy, anger management, and AA."

Maggie was awed and humbled by Pastor David's dedication to helping someone she was sure many would write off as a lost cause. "He does go the extra mile, doesn't he? I have the feeling if I say no, I'll feel slightly less than Christian."

"No no," Liz hastened to assure her. "Do what you feel comfortable with, Maggie. I'm not trying to twist your arm."

Maggie smiled. How could she refuse with the wonderful example the Youngs set? "I'll see you in ten."

Maggie easily found a spot in front of the white clapboard building located down on the waterfront with a good view of the harbor. She supposed crime fighting in a Maine coastal town could easily involve boats and the water in addition to misdeeds committed on land.

Inside the station, the desk clerk, Paula Ellis, looked up from her computer. The half dozen or so desks behind her were empty, although one still had a reading light switched on.

"Good evening, Maggie," Paula said. "Here to see Officer Linton? I'm afraid he and Janeen are out on patrol. Do you need me to call them back for you?"

"That's a good assumption, but I'm actually not here to see

Officer Linton for once. My friend Liz Young called me and asked me to come down and speak to Cody Becker."

Paula's face looked doubtful. "Becker?" She swiveled in her chair and called out, "Hey, Samantha?"

Officer Samantha Clayton entered the main room at the back. "What's up, Paula?" Tall and rangy, Somerset Harbor native Samantha Clayton gave the impression of strength and grace. Maggie could easily imagine her working on a lobster boat like her father and brothers.

"Maggie's here to see Becker."

Samantha nodded. "Oh yeah. The Youngs said that she would be stopping by."

"Aren't they here?" Maggie asked in dismay. She had pictured them standing by and offering support, although Liz hadn't exactly said that.

"They wanted to stay, but Pastor David got a call from the hospital. Critical patient." Samantha beckoned to her. "Let's go back. We have a few minutes before supper is served, so your timing is perfect."

In response to the mention of supper, Maggie's stomach rumbled. After her visit with Cody, she'd stop by The Golden Chopsticks and get takeout. Otherwise she wouldn't have time to eat before the meeting.

Paula unlocked the gate so Maggie could enter the station's inner sanctum. She wove her way through the desks to the back hallway, which led to the chief's office and break room one way and to the holding cells the other way.

"It will be all right." Samantha gave her a sympathetic face. "He won't bite, not on my watch."

"Is it that obvious?"

Samantha chuckled. "Yeah. You look petrified."

Cody Becker was sitting on his bunk, head down and hands

hanging between his knees. He looked up when he heard their footsteps on the polished tile. "Ms. Watson. You came."

Against my better judgment. "I did." She stopped several feet away from the bars enclosing the young man.

Samantha pulled up a folding chair for her. "Have a seat. I'll be within earshot right around the corner. Ten minutes, okay? Mr. Becker's supper should be arriving then." The officer gave Cody a glare. "Lucky you, getting takeout on the taxpayer's dime." To Maggie, she said, "We don't have a kitchen, so we have to order the inmates' food from the local restaurants."

Cody's head dropped. "I'm sorry for causing you the hassle."

"Stay out of trouble in the future, then." Samantha turned crisply on her heel and strode out, leaving Maggie alone with the prisoner.

Maggie settled herself into the hard molded chair, wishing with all her heart she was somewhere else—anywhere else—right now. Cody was silent, one elbow propped on a knee while he contemplated his unlaced sneakers.

"What did you want to talk to me about?" Maggie finally asked after the silence stretched to an unendurable length, although only two minutes had passed according to her cell phone.

Cody looked up, his bloodshot eyes meeting hers directly. "It's hard to talk about. I wanted to, but now that you're here, I . . . I feel stupid."

Studying his youthful face, which hadn't settled into the final lines of adulthood yet, Maggie felt a pang of compassion. He reminded her of Emily's friends, maybe one who had taken a terribly wrong turn. He should be with friends, setting up a bright future, not sitting in a jail cell.

"Don't worry about feeling stupid. What counts is what you do from now on, not what happened in the past."

Cody's face brightened a degree. "That's what Pastor David said. He actually gave me the idea that I could turn my life around."

"Of course you can. No one can do it for you."

"I suppose." Cody lifted one shoulder. Without turning his head, he darted beady eyes at Maggie. "I'm sorry for scaring you the other night."

"Which time are you talking about?" The night he accosted her outside the town hall or the night he lurked in the shadows, watching the historical society? Or maybe he had scratched at the office window and left the threatening notes.

"You get scared a lot? That stinks." A glint of amusement crossed his sullen face. "I mean when I came up on you like that outside the town hall. And for how I acted at the Quadrille and The Bean."

Maggie realized something disturbing. Unless Cody was refusing to confess to the other incidents for some reason, someone else was trying to frighten her and warn her off. "Outside the town hall is the only time you tried to scare me, Cody?"

He put up one hand. "Yep. Honest. And that was an accident. I was just trying to get ahold of Mackenzie. She's not speaking to me for some reason."

Maggie cocked her head. "The first time I saw you, you were shaking her. And those other times you mentioned, you acted threatening. No wonder she doesn't want to talk to you."

A red tide moved up his neck. "I know, I know. I'm excitable. And I have a bad temper. That's why Pastor David wants me to go to anger management classes."

"Good idea. But don't count on mending fences with Mackenzie. I mean, she moved up here instead of staying near you in Boston."

"First, let me say this. I care about Mackenzie—a lot. I'm torn up inside about how things have gone down between us. I know it doesn't look like I do, but believe me, she's about my best friend in the world. My only friend."

"Then you need to cherish her, not hurt her." Maggie heard

the condemning note creep into her voice. But really, he needed to face reality.

He nodded decisively. "You're right. And I'm going to make it up to her, once I find her." He fastened hopeful eyes on her. "Maybe you can help me."

"I'm not going to encourage her to see you, Cody. I'll pass along your message, that's all."

"I understand." He fell silent, the tapping of one foot his only movement.

"Good luck, Cody. I wish you well." Maggie shifted in her seat, preparing to stand up and leave.

"Mackenzie said she was onto something big. That's why she moved up here."

"What do you mean?"

He shook his head. "She didn't tell me the details. Something to do with her family." He made the universal gesture of rubbing fingers together, referring to money. "Someone has big bucks."

Maggie studied the young man for a moment, her thoughts whirling. What he was saying didn't fit with the Mackenzie she knew. The young woman had presented herself as innocently inquiring into a possible connection with her family's past.

A terrible idea wormed its way into her brain. What if Mackenzie had come here just to find some supposed relatives to latch onto? Someone like Ruby Adams, elderly and alone, would be extremely vulnerable to such manipulation.

Her mind flipped through the mysterious events plaguing her over the past week. The threatening notes. The missing photographs at the lighthouse and Ruby's house. The stolen quilt blocks. It wasn't much of a stretch to theorize that Mackenzie might be responsible. But why? What was she hoping to gain?

Maggie stood, clutching her churning stomach with one hand. Had her new friend deceived them all?

18

Instead of Chinese food, which suddenly sounded too controversial for her stomach, Maggie stopped by the Lobster Quadrille for a bowl of clam chowder. She worried that even the lobster bisque wouldn't sit well. Besides, not only did she need a little nourishment, but she also needed a chance to sit quietly and sort through her thoughts before the historical society meeting, where she might see Mackenzie.

Sitting alone in the bustling restaurant as she waited for her soup, with the classic voices of Frank Sinatra and Dean Martin crooning over the sound system, Maggie felt herself relax. She was glad her chat with Cody had been short and she actually had time to soak in the comforting atmosphere of the restaurant. She attempted to think through her situation, but her mind skittered away from all thoughts of Mackenzie, the quilt blocks, and every single strange event. She needed a break, a mental pause during which she could gather fresh energy and insight.

The server had just brought her bowl of soup and oyster crackers when a familiar figure entered the front door — Adrian Diaz. A reporter was the last person she wanted to talk to right now. She sat back, hoping a broad-backed gentleman seated in front of her would block Adrian's view, but no such luck.

He headed right for her with a wave. "Hey, Maggie. How's it going?"

"Hi Adrian. Are you covering the historical society meeting tonight?"

"I am. I thought I'd stop by for a quick bite first."

She felt compelled by politeness to ask him to join her. "Have a seat. I'm just getting started."

He put his hand on the back of the chair opposite and pulled it out. "If you don't mind. I was planning on getting a fish sandwich to go, but eating it here is much nicer." He checked his phone. "And it looks like we still have plenty of time before the meeting."

A wave to the server brought her back over and Adrian placed his order. "Tell me," he said, dark eyes twinkling with an expression of avid curiosity. "Any sign of the missing quilt blocks?"

So much for avoiding the topic. "I'm afraid not. How did you know about them anyway?"

Adrian thanked the server for the coffee she placed in front of him, then added two sugars and stirred. "Part of my beat is reading the police reports. I saw the entry Officer Linton made after the visit to Fran's shop." He shook his head. "The quilt blocks aren't exactly a hot item. I wonder why the thief wanted them."

Words crowded Maggie's lips, exclamations regarding the theft of the blocks and the other small thefts and harassments. But she knew better than to confide in a reporter. That was one sure way to lose control of a situation, not that she seemed to be able to stem the tide of odd incidents or even figure out for sure who was responsible. She preferred the perpetrator—or perpetrators—to remain in the dark regarding her thoughts and actions. They were her only cards and she planned on keeping them close to her vest.

She took a sip of soup, then forced herself to say casually, "I have no idea. According to Fran, their worth is mainly sentimental, although assembled vintage quilts can sell for good money."

Adrian snorted. "I wonder who would even fence something like that. Can you imagine a black market in old linens?"

His comment made Maggie chortle. "That does sound absurd."

Anyway, she believed the motive for the theft was personal, not business, but she wasn't about to discuss that with Adrian. She eyed the plate the server delivered. "That looks good."

"Sure does." Adrian tucked into his fried fish on a bun and generous heap of crispy fries. "Help yourself to the French fries." After a few bites, he asked, "Any news on the lighthouse?"

Relieved that the topic had moved to something less awkward, Maggie filled him in on her visit out there with James. "You should contact him for the details once he comes up with an estimate."

"I'll do that." Adrian's cell went off with an insistent buzz. He perused the screen. "Uh-oh. I've got to go. There's a big fire on Route 1 outside of town."

"Does that mean you'll miss the historical society meeting?" She tried to keep relief out of her voice. Now she could talk to her friends without everything she said ending up on the front page.

"I'm afraid so. Ask Ruth to send me the minutes, will you?" Adrian waved down their server. "Can I get a box?"

Maggie hoped no one was hurt, but as she watched the young reporter dash out of the restaurant, she'd never been so grateful to hear about a fire.

. . . .

"You've outdone yourself with the baked goods," Maggie said to Daisy a short while later at the historical society meeting, gesturing at the two large platters on the table next to the coffee and tea urns. There were apricot and raspberry bars, lemon tarts, and an array of cookies that included chocolate chunk, oatmeal-cranberry, and good old white chocolate–macadamia nut.

Daisy selected an oatmeal cookie with the tongs and put it on a paper plate. "I heard it was going to be a long meeting, so I thought I'd make sure we were well fortified."

Maggie reflected on all that had happened since their dinner at the Quadrille. *Long meeting, indeed.* "I think you're right." She loaded a couple of treats onto her own plate. "Do you know if Mackenzie's coming tonight?"

"I don't think so. She and Jenny had plans to go bowling." Daisy smiled. "Bowling is popular again—do you believe it? All the kids like retro activities these days."

Maggie hid her relief at Mackenzie's absence under a chuckle. She wasn't ready to see or talk to her yet. "They do say everything comes back in style."

Ruth was calling the meeting to order, so Maggie and Daisy hurried to find seats.

"First order of discussion is the lighthouse project," Ruth said. "I'm pleased to report that the Lighthouse Heritage Foundation will give us a matching grant of up to $20,000. That means for every dollar we raise, they give us a dollar, up to $20,000."

Everyone burst into applause, with Ina adding a whoop or two while stamping her feet. Maggie smiled. She admired Ina's no-holds-barred approach to life, in response to both the good and the bad.

"They felt the Somerset Harbor Lighthouse was significant and worthy of support," Ruth said once the clapping died down.

"Darn tootin' it is," Ina said.

"This is wonderful news," Liz Young said. "That grant will double the money we raise."

"I wonder if $40,000 will be enough," June said. "Do we have any idea about the costs yet?"

"Not quite," Maggie said. "James Bennett and I went out to the lighthouse this morning, and he's working on an estimate." She pulled the notes she'd made out of her tote. "I do have notes concerning what James said today."

"Go ahead and share that, if you don't mind," Ruth said.

Maggie read through the list. "James did say the foundation was sound and most of the brickwork intact, which means stonemasonry costs should be minimal."

"I had my chimney repointed last year and it wasn't cheap," June said, "so that's a huge relief."

"It sounds like we might need replacement windows," Liz said. "But maybe the old ones can be restored. We had someone fix the window frames at the church so we could keep the original windows. I can give James the name of that company if that's what we want to do."

"That sounds good, Liz," Maggie said. "James said he'd figure out prices both for replacement and restoration for different areas of the building, with the main goal being maintaining the character of the lighthouse."

"Let's all help pull the workers and materials together to keep the costs down," Daisy said.

"Any other comments?" Ruth asked. After a pause, she said, "Thanks for that report, Maggie. June, is there any other news about fundraising?"

"I got the word today that the lighthouse was chosen as the beneficiary of funds raised at the Oceanview Hotel Valentine's Day dinner," June said. "That should net us a couple thousand."

Again, clapping and cheers broke out.

"Great job, June," Ruth said. "Anyone have anything else to report? No? All right, Maggie, where are we on the quilt block project?"

"Well," Maggie began, "I have good news and bad news." The group listened with rapt attention as she detailed the events of the past few days. She didn't mention Cody's revelations about Mackenzie. She wanted to talk to Mackenzie in private first.

"So in summary," Ina said, "we've found two Sarahs, but we aren't sure if any of them were Mackenzie's great-great-grandmother yet. And we lost the blocks and a couple of photographs, but found the original sketches made by the other Sarah, the one who disappeared. Do I have that straight?"

"That's about the size of it," Maggie said. "There's also this." She pulled the bullet, safely enclosed in a plastic sandwich bag, and displayed it to the group. "James pried this out of a hutch from Sarah Monroe's dining room today."

Ina, sitting next to Maggie, took the bag and peered at its contents. "Is this a bullet?" She passed it to June, next in line.

"We think so." At Maggie's words, several people gasped.

"Does this mean Sarah Monroe was shot?" Fran's nose wrinkled in disgust. "What a horrible family."

Liz stared at Fran. "You think a family member did it?"

Maggie understood Fran's perspective, but she wasn't going to divulge her friend's complicated relationship with a present-day Monroe. "Fran has a point. If it had been an outsider, her father would have reported it to the police. Why cover it up?"

Ina shifted forward in her chair, her eyes avid. "I get the picture now. At dinner that cold February night, Sarah tells her father that she won't marry the banker. Furious, Horace picks up his revolver and fires." Ina jumped to her feet and mimed pulling the trigger of a gun. "One bullet goes into the hutch and, tragically" — Ina gripped her chest — "another pierces the heart of his precious daughter. Horace, remorseful and panicking, doesn't know what to do. But the banker, who arrives at that moment, helps Horace carry Sarah's body to the lighthouse. They toss her over the cliff, letting the sea claim her." Ina threw out her arms as if casting a heavy load. "Then they leave her scarf so everyone thinks she killed herself or ran away." She sat triumphantly.

"Hold on there, Ina," Daisy said. "It might have been an accident. Horace could've been cleaning his gun and it went off."

"Or there was an argument over a game of cards and Sarah wasn't even involved," June suggested.

"Maybe someone scared off a burglar," Liz put in.

"I know what happened," came a quiet voice. Everyone turned to Deborah Bennett, who until now hadn't said a word. She usually seemed content to sit back and listen to the others chatter. Now, as they all gaped at her, she smiled smugly and patted the worn leather book cradled in her lap. "I've been waiting for the right moment to share the real story of Sarah Monroe."

"Well, tell it, woman!" Ina wagged an admonishing finger. "We're dying of curiosity over here."

Deborah was apparently enjoying the suspense. "In due time. I suggest all of you get fresh cups of coffee and more cookies. It's a long story."

Seeing that she had no intention of divulging the story before she was ready, the other women of the historical society obeyed. They settled back in their chairs with additional sustenance and the shivery expectation of a fascinating story shared on a long, cold winter night.

"Well now," said Deborah. "Remember I told you I found Priscilla Allen's diary? At first it was fairly boring—accounts of the weather and household affairs and such—but in a certain month of a certain year, things got . . . interesting." She paused and looked at their faces. Apparently Deborah Bennett had a flair for the dramatic too.

Ina bounced in her chair. "February 1898?"

"That's right. The month Sarah Monroe vanished." Deborah opened the diary, adjusted her glasses and began to read.

It is with barely suppressed excitement that I record the following, the story of how the stalwart ladies of the Somerset Harbor Quilting Guild assisted one of our own to escape oppression and calamity. In this day and age, at the end of the nineteenth century for pity's sake, why do some men persist in treating women as possessions, fit only to be bartered for wealth and position?

It was obvious to Maggie that Priscilla was referring to Sarah Monroe's situation with the arranged marriage. How had the quilting guild helped her escape?

I digress—something my darling Charles accuses me of doing quite frequently. We couldn't have pulled off our scheme without his help. Thank goodness all men aren't cut from the same cloth. Anyway, our dear sister came to us at the January meeting of our little group with a terrible report. For some time, her father had been allowing an older man to press his suit, favoring the marriage the man proposed. Our friend resisted for many reasons. The man is an ill-mannered boor, he is much older and extremely corpulent, and he has a reputation for being cruel. What's more, she was in love with another, a man without much money but with bright prospects.

Aha! Another man. Maggie waited impatiently for the story to unfold in Priscilla's own good time. And Deborah's.

There was a young doctor who had traveled to Somerset Harbor on vacation. He met our friend on the cliffs, where she was painting at the time. Her work is wonderful and is in fact the basis for our latest project, an album quilt, which we planned to give to our dear friend.

The quilt blocks! Maggie thought triumphantly.

A friendship swiftly sprang up. Over the course of the summer, something more grew from it. She had found the man she wanted to marry. But her father would hear nothing of it. In fact, the only time John came to the house, her father actually fired a weapon to scare him off.

The patriarch threatened to report John to the authorities under a false claim that he wasn't fit to be licensed as a physician. He had enough power to ruin the young man's life, and his daughter begged him not to carry out such a cruel act.

John left town soon after, and to all appearances the summer romance was dead, fled with the warm weather. But underneath, coals still glowed, and our young lady was determined to marry John. They corresponded in secret, and in January, she came to us to beg for our help. Her father had set a date for her wedding to the dreadful bank officer, and she was desperate.

The guild helped create a plan and each woman played a part, all different but essential.

Deborah broke off her reading. "Listen up, ladies—this is where it gets good."

"Just now?" Ina quipped.

I hosted a dinner party for the patriarch and the banker, along with my darling Charles, under pretense of congratulating them on the match. However, on the day of the party, our own Sarah Anne Stewart, a nurse, made the diagnosis that our friend was contagious with a bout of influenza and could not attend the event.

Daisy gripped Maggie's arm. "That's Harry's ancestor."

Our dear Julia Sedgwick and the minister's wife, Emily Braddock, had arranged a small and secret wedding at Sedgwick Manor, to be officiated by Pastor Braddock.

Maggie felt a surge of pride at this evidence of her relative's loyalty to a friend. "*Sometimes being a friend means keeping a secret*," she quoted. "My aunt Evelyn wrote that in the description of the blocks. Now we know what she meant."

Nellie Linton kept watch with her telescope. Another took our friend's favorite scarf to the lighthouse and left it on top of the cliffs, to give the impression that Sarah had come to a bitter end. It wasn't safe for her to tell her father the truth. He would have tracked her down ruthlessly. Others watched the roads and the harbor, where the couple would flee on a ship to John's home in Boston. Sarah Anne's fiancé had arranged the transport.

Maggie felt a rising hum of excitement. She was almost certain she knew who John was.

Everything went seamlessly. The couple was wed and on their way out to sea by the time the dinner party was over, with no one the wiser save our little group. Sarah Monroe is now Mrs. John Floyd, on her way to a new life with the man she loves. We didn't have a chance to finish the quilt we were making for her. Julia sent her quilt block with the Floyds, as something to remember us by, and stores the rest of the blocks in Sedgwick Manor, to be assembled and given to our dear friend should we see her again in this life.

Several people gasped at the sheer romance of the story.

"I guess that means Sarah Monroe was Mackenzie's great-great-grandmother." For a moment, Maggie felt a thrill at solving the mystery, at the news that Mackenzie did indeed have family in Somerset Harbor. But then Cody's words replayed in her mind, as jarring as spotting a worm in a pristine apple. "She was on to something big," he had said. Did that mean Mackenzie had known that Sarah Monroe was her ancestor before coming to town? If so, what game was she playing with Tyler Monroe? With an effort, Maggie returned her attention to the group.

"How wonderful," Liz was saying. "Sarah Monroe didn't die after all."

"At least not then," Ina said, ever practical.

"So the quilting guild all knew the story and never shared it with anyone?" June asked. "That is quite a feat for over a dozen women."

Deborah's face was somber. "There's a little more to the story. You see, that night there was a terrible, sudden blizzard that engulfed the entire East Coast. According to the diary, Priscilla believed that Sarah's boat might have been lost at sea, as dozens of others were. But because of their pact never to communicate, the friends never knew for certain if Sarah and John perished on their wedding night."

Now the gasps and groans were poignant, but Daisy patted her chest. "We know there was a happy ending. Otherwise Mackenzie wouldn't be here. If only the quilting guild could have known that too."

There was another moment of silence, but then Ina rubbed her hands together in glee. "Who's going to spill the beans to Miss Mackenzie Floyd?"

"We could call her right now," June said. "Who has her number?"

"I do," Daisy said. "I have all my employees on speed dial." She pulled her cell phone out of her bag and placed the call. A few seconds later, she shook her head. "Right to voice mail." She left a brief message asking Mackenzie to call when she had a chance. "It's getting late, so I doubt I'll hear from her tonight."

"You'll see her at The Bean tomorrow, won't you, Daisy?" Liz said.

"Actually, she's off tomorrow, so probably not." Daisy turned to Maggie. "I think you should tell her. You're closest to her, and I think she'd appreciate it coming from you."

A day ago Maggie would have agreed heartily with Daisy's assessment of her relationship with the young woman. But now, maybe Mackenzie still felt close to her, but she felt the opposite, as if she really didn't know the young woman at all. Well, there was only one way to find out; she would have to confront her. "Sure, I'll do that. I'll give her a call and ask her to come by the house tomorrow."

"Good idea," Ina said. "News like that should be delivered in person." Then she snickered. "I'm getting such a kick out of imagining Nellie Linton keeping watch with her telescope."

"That is quite a picture," Daisy said. "I can't wait to tell Harry his great-grandmother's role in the whole story either."

"I can understand you're all eager to share," Ruth said, "but please, don't breathe a word about Sarah Monroe until Maggie has a chance to tell Mackenzie. You know this town—she'll get the news in about five minutes. And Mackenzie will have her hands full after the news breaks."

Liz sighed. "I guess we'll have to keep the quilting guild's secret one more day."

"What's one day to over a hundred years?" Ina craned her neck toward the cookies. "I guess I'll have one for the road, but then I'd really like to get home and hit the rack."

"I take it that's a hint the meeting's over," Ruth said. "All right then. Do I hear a motion to adjourn?"

Maggie drove Ina home and then headed for the mansion with relief. Once again it had been an extremely long and varied day, including a nice trip to the lighthouse with James, a visit to the jail, and the revelation of the true story behind Sarah Monroe's disappearance. No wonder her head felt like it was spinning.

Fortunately for her nerves, she didn't see any strange vehicles tailing her on the short distance home. The driveway was empty and the front door clean of any nasty notes. Snickers came padding to greet her, his reproachful meow seeming to question why she had been gone so long.

She bent to pat him. "I know, I know. Hopefully things will calm down soon and we can spend some quality time napping. Or you can nap and I'll read in front of the fire. How does that sound?" His loud purr sounded like approval.

Maggie stood and shed her outdoor garments. It was almost ten o'clock according to the grandfather clock near the stairs. Too late to call Mackenzie, but she could send a text. She'd have to play it by ear from there.

Maybe she would finally learn the truth about Mackenzie Floyd.

19

When Maggie awoke the next morning, she was conscious of a warm hum of anticipation in her belly. Then she remembered. Tonight was the Valentine's Day dinner at the Oceanview.

She reached over and stroked Snickers, who lay curled up beside her. In response, he rolled over and exposed his belly. "Think I'll have fun tonight, Snickers?" His answer was a rumbling purr. "I hope you're right."

Throwing back the covers, Maggie went to the window to open the drapes and check on the weather. To her dismay, lacy snowflakes drifted down from a cast-iron sky. "Snow again? I hope it doesn't interfere with tonight's dinner." That was one of the main drawbacks of living in New England: Bad winter weather could cancel the best-laid plans.

Tying on a robe, she went to the kitchen to start coffee, and then checked the weather report on her laptop. To her relief, the forecast was calling for flurries on and off but no major accumulation. She'd left her cell phone on the table beside her computer the night before, and she picked it up to see if she had any messages.

Mackenzie hadn't texted back, which was really strange. *Should I send her another message?* Indecisive, she stood holding the phone, debating whether it was too soon to follow up. When the phone chimed, she almost dropped it and fumbled to answer.

"Good morning, June. What's on the agenda today?"

Even at this early hour, June's voice was cheerful and brisk. "That's what I wanted to talk to you about. I thought I'd help you price Tyler Monroe's bedroom furniture so you can give him a quote. And maybe finish that inventory."

"Sounds great. See you in a bit?" Maggie was still learning the ropes at the antiques business. While she was developing an eye for quality and value, she was uneasy about pricing items. She was afraid to pay too much or sell for too little. June's mentorship was invaluable.

"Sure thing. Want me to stop for muffins? I heard Daisy say she was making morning glory muffins today."

"That sounds great. Thanks." After disconnecting, Maggie poured herself a cup of coffee and went back to the bedroom to drink it. Feeling incredibly lazy and decadent, she propped herself against the pillows and read for a while, the cat snoozing beside her.

At moments like this, she realized how much she enjoyed her new home. Not wanting worry or stress to mar her peace, she resolved to put aside the mysteries plaguing her and just enjoy the day. Tomorrow was soon enough to figure out what was going on.

Though she wished Mackenzie would text her back.

. . . .

At six o'clock sharp that evening, the front doorbell rang. She hurried for the front door, patting her hair in place as she went. Tonight she wore a little more makeup than usual, and she was aware of the light trail of perfume that followed her, something she rarely indulged in.

James's eyes widened when she opened the door. "Wow—I mean, good evening, Maggie." A broad grin broke across his face. "You're looking lovely tonight."

Maggie shrugged into her red wool coat, the one she wore for special occasions. "You look nice too." She admiringly took in his long black overcoat and charcoal wool dress pants, his polished boots and sleek leather gloves. She'd never seen James so formally attired, and it suited him, despite the bruising on his cheek from Cody's punch.

She wore boots so as not to soil her pumps with salt and snow, but James kept a steadying hand under her elbow anyway as she descended the porch steps and made her way to his car, where he opened the door for her. A joke rose to her lips at this shift in their relationship, but she bit it back, sensing that he enjoyed his role as courtly gentleman. Tomorrow they would probably revert back to the old Maggie and James, but tonight was special and there was nothing wrong with that.

"I've never been to the Oceanview, you know," she said as he maneuvered the car through the quiet streets. Light snow began to fall again, as it had on and off all day.

"You're in for a treat then," he said, glancing over with a smile. "Their chef is one of the best on the Maine coast."

At the sprawling, Victorian-era hotel, James pulled up under the porte cochere, where a bundled-up valet offered to park the Mercedes. Maggie was grateful they didn't have to traipse across the wide, cold parking lot; she could see the Oceanview was packed already, even though they were still early. She was glad she had had the foresight to change into her pumps and leave her boots in the car so she didn't have to carry the bulky things all night.

They entered through double doors into the spacious lobby, which had a beamed ceiling, polished floorboards adorned with Oriental rugs, and traditional furniture placed in conversational groupings. Tiny white lights embellished windows and doorways, the staircase bannister, and potted trees, providing a festive air. Bouquets of red roses placed on side tables and the grand piano released their sweet scent into the warm air.

To the left was the long front desk, where a clerk greeted them pleasantly. "Here for the Valentine's dinner? You're welcome to have a drink in the lounge, or you may proceed right to the dining room."

"Want to go to the lounge first?" James asked. "It's a nice place."

"Sure. Why not?"

James pulled a small box out of a deep pocket of his overcoat. "By the way, I have something for you."

"What is it?"

"A corsage." He opened the lid to reveal a delicate white orchid. She gasped. "It's beautiful. You didn't have to."

"I wanted to."

She held very still as he pinned the flower to her blouse. When was the last time she had worn a corsage? Once he finished, she gazed admiringly at it and stroked the velvety petals. "Thank you."

He held out his hand to help her rise. "You're welcome." His eyes shone as he looked at her.

The lounge was a cozy, wood-paneled room with a huge fire in a fieldstone fireplace. A moose head mounted above kept watch over the guests. They sat at a small table just inside the door, and James went to the bar to order two glasses of wine.

Maggie scanned the merry crowd, hoping to spot someone she knew. However, she wrinkled her nose when she succeeded. On the other side of the room, she spotted Tyler Monroe, handsome in tie and suit jacket. The woman he was with was facing the other way; all Maggie could see was short dark hair and the low-cut back of her red dress, but she knew who it was. Mackenzie.

Unease panged when she thought about the young woman spending time with such a scheming man. Then she had another thought: Weren't they cousins of sorts? And what if Tyler was the less conniving of the two after all?

"Here you are." James set a glass of wine gently in front of Maggie so as not to spill it. "Sorry it took so long. They're slammed."

"That's all right," Maggie said. Thoughts of Mackenzie drifted away as James sat down with his own glass. Tonight she would concentrate on her companion.

After enjoying conversation and wine, they moved to the dining room and sat at a table along the wall overlooking the bay. On an overcast night, there wasn't much of a view, but the twinkling lights from houses along the shoreline were pretty.

"This is really nice," Maggie said, admiring the white table-cloth, sprinkling of red rose petals, and burning candle floating in a bowl of water. The silverware was heavy and lustrous, the glasses crystal. A small orchestra in the corner played romantic favorites at low volume.

"I agree. This is one of my favorite events ever." James greeted the server, who bowed slightly as he presented a printed menu panel to each of them.

"Good evening. I'm Marc, and I'll be taking care of you this evening."

Maggie checked out the menu, which was prix fixe. "We can pick whatever we want from this list?" She had expected a standard banquet-type meal, which was preplanned.

"That's right—one item from each category. Let's get started on the salads, and then I'll be back for the rest of your order."

"I'll have the mixed greens, goat cheese, and walnut salad with raspberry vinaigrette," she said.

James echoed her order. After Marc promised to have them right out, Maggie set to work studying the options. "Oh, this is fabulous. Shrimp scampi, seared scallops, and prime rib?" She didn't bother to consider the fettuccine alfredo or the coq au vin. She could eat cheesy pasta or chicken any day.

"I'm thinking prime rib," James said. "Theirs melts in your mouth."

"I'm having the scallops. Maybe we can share." A blush heated her cheeks at this suggestion but James chuckled and agreed.

"Surf and turf, my favorite."

Someone bumped the back of Maggie's chair, and she turned to see Mackenzie being seated at the next table along with Tyler, who nodded a greeting.

Mackenzie put one hand to her mouth. "Whoops, I'm sorry! I'm such a klutz whenever I wear heels." She held up one foot, displaying four-inch stilettos. The action pushed her short dress higher; she tugged the hem back down, giggling.

Was there a slight slur in Mackenzie's voice? And why hadn't she called Maggie by name? "That's okay, Mackenzie. Enjoy your meal." Maggie turned back to James, but she was viscerally aware of the couple behind them. In contrast to the murmuring couples around them, they were hard to ignore, especially Mackenzie, who grew more rambunctious as dinner went on.

"You're really going to eat that, Tyler? I never saw so much blood come out of a piece of meat."

Maggie looked at James, who grimaced as he cut into his prime rib. "I guess I'm a proud carnivore," he muttered.

"Me too," Maggie said, accepting the bite he offered her. *Yum.* It melted, just as James had promised. The garlic mashed potatoes—perfectly browned on top—were also divine.

"Get me another drink, will you, Marc? And take away these scallops. Ugh. Dry and rubbery!" Mackenzie's voice was so loud that people from neighboring tables turned to stare.

Marc paused at their table, still holding Mackenzie's plate. "How are the scallops, ma'am?" he whispered to Maggie.

"Delectable. Really." She pointed at her empty plate as proof, leaning back so he could take it away.

"I've heard alcohol can affect the taste buds," James said in an undertone.

The server beamed. "Thank you. I'll bring the dessert menu by in a jiffy."

From his seat, James could see Mackenzie and Tyler clearly, and by the disturbed expression on his face, Maggie guessed things were going downhill fast.

"What is it?" she said, leaning across the table.

"Mackenzie just laid her head on the table." He shook his head. "I think she's . . . passed out."

At this confirmation of her own fears, Maggie turned in her seat. Tyler was on his feet, attempting to rouse Mackenzie. "Come on, sweetie. Time to go."

"Do you need some help?" Maggie offered.

Tyler threw her a terse smile. "No no. I can handle it." He managed to get the young woman out of the chair and up on her feet, then half-walked, half-dragged her along the carpet.

Marc arrived back at their table with the promised menus, and the three of them watched as Mackenzie and Tyler staggered out of the dining room. "Marc, that young woman is a friend of mine," Maggie said to the waiter. "Can you tell me what she was drinking?"

"Yes ma'am. The strange thing is, she wasn't drinking alcohol, only diet soda." He handed them the menus with a sigh. "She must have started early somewhere else. Maybe she had some in the lounge."

Maggie tried to focus on the dessert menu, but her mind was full of worry. She chose the lava cake, yet she kept seeing Mackenzie being practically carried out of the room, seemingly intoxicated. If she wasn't drunk, as Marc claimed, then what was wrong with her? Had Tyler slipped her something so he could take advantage of her? Maggie hoped not.

Then it hit her. Had Tyler learned that Mackenzie was his long-lost relative and had a more direct line to his mansion's original owner than he did? Maybe he wasn't happy about the prospect of sharing his wealth. Her heart began to hammer. Every instinct in her body screamed that Mackenzie was in trouble.

James put his napkin on the table. "Can you excuse me for a minute?"

"Of course." She assumed he was headed for the restroom. Then she noticed another man walking in that direction, someone she hadn't recognized at first in his shirt and tie, despite his bushy red beard. It was Jed Parker. "Do me a favor, James? Ask Jed what color the pickup is that Tyler 'stole' from him."

He gave her a strange look but nodded. "Be right back."

Maggie toyed with her cake while she waited for his return. Her thoughts and nerves howled for her to do something, but she couldn't move, constrained by the decorum of a social event. Outside, the falling snow thickened, gusting in bursts of flakes that melted on the window. *Great, another storm.*

"Jed said the truck was white," James said as he sat across from her again. "Are you going to tell me why you're interested?" His eyes were teasing. "I was thinking of asking you to dance, not discussing vehicles." Several couples were already on the dance floor, moving slowly to the love songs the orchestra continued to play.

Maggie barely heard the invitation. *Tyler owned a white truck.* All the pieces fell into place. The hit-and-run, the tailgating, the man watching from the trees outside the historical society . . . Tyler Monroe was responsible for it all. No doubt he had also vandalized the newspapers and stolen the photographs, all to prevent Mackenzie—or anyone else—from learning the truth.

"James, I'm so sorry, but we've got to leave. I'm having a wonderful time, but I think it could be a matter of life or death." If she was wrong, then she was the worst kind of fool, ruining such a perfect evening. But she couldn't take the chance of another Monroe heiress vanishing—this time due to foul play.

20

············

Maggie's whole body was tense as she sat in the passenger seat beside James, as if her efforts could make them move faster. "I'd like nothing more than to find out she really did just drink too much. But something's telling me there's more to the story."

"Which way?" James asked.

"Let's go by her apartment first. If she was sick, Tyler should have taken her there. She lives above The Golden Chopsticks on Broad."

"Right." James buzzed along the side streets despite the deepening snow. In front of the restaurant, James stopped the car in the middle of the street since there wasn't any other traffic. Lights still glowed in the eatery, but all the apartments above were dark.

Maggie scanned the cars parked along the street. "I don't see Tyler's BMW anywhere."

"Is there a parking lot behind the building?" James edged the car forward. "Oh I see it." He pulled into an alley that led around the back. A few cars sat there, some of which were covered with snow, meaning they hadn't moved for a while. No BMW.

The tension in Maggie's belly tightened. "He must have taken her to his house." She didn't want to think about what that might mean.

"The Monroe Mansion it is," James said grimly. Another alley at the other end brought them back out onto the street, and James turned for the mansion.

They raced past familiar buildings with James driving at the perfect speed to maximize progress while maintaining control on the increasingly slippery roads. When Monroe Mansion loomed out of the dark, Maggie's pulse ratcheted up even higher. What would they discover at the mansion? Dreadful pictures tried to enter her mind, but she blocked them forcibly. No, she needed to concentrate on the goal—getting Mackenzie out of there safely.

"Aha, they're here," James said with grim satisfaction. The headlights revealed fresh tire tracks heading into the driveway. He turned in and slowed, creeping along the narrow lane. No lights shone from the three-story house ahead.

Maggie remembered from their previous visit that the driveway branched, one way going toward the house to form a circular drive, the other toward the barn. To her surprise, the way toward the house lay pristine and untouched by traffic.

"He didn't pull up to the house," she said. "How strange."

"Maybe he parked in the barn." James turned right, toward the outbuilding. Here they found Tyler's BMW huddled under a rapidly building cover of snow. James braked sharply and turned off the engine. But as he and Maggie got out of the car, she noticed something.

"I don't think they're here after all." She pointed to the barn door, which stood open. "Look, there are tire tracks leading away from the barn. He must have taken her somewhere in the truck."

James groaned. "They could be anywhere. We'll never find them before the snow covers their tracks." The white flakes were already erasing the tire tracks that led away from the barn.

Where are they, Lord? To the south, a wide beam swept across the horizon, lighting the underbelly of the clouds.

With a jolt, she realized where they were—and why. She ran for the car. "James, we've got to get to the lighthouse! Hurry!"

"Tell me again what's going on?" James was forced to drive more slowly against the driving snow buffeting the car. Out here on the cliffs, the wind was brutal.

"Mackenzie is Sarah Monroe's great-great-granddaughter. Priscilla Allen's diary said that Sarah didn't die at the lighthouse.

She ran away and married John Floyd, a doctor from Massachusetts—Mackenzie's great-great-grandfather."

"My mother has Priscilla's diary? Why didn't I hear about it?"

"I'm sorry. We all decided to keep it a secret until we could tell Mackenzie. I thought about telling you tonight, but I didn't want to spoil the mood by talking about historical society business."

"I don't think it would have spoiled the mood, but I understand. So why would that upset Tyler? Doesn't it mean he and Mackenzie are related?" He made a face. "And they were out on a date. Ugh."

"They are distant relatives, but listen, James. Sarah Monroe was the direct heir of the Monroe fortune and house. Tyler is from another branch of the family. I bet Mackenzie could claim everything, once she proves she is a direct descendant. If Tyler knows who she is, then he'll have figured that out too."

James's expression went very still. "I get it." He stepped on the gas, then backed off when the car fishtailed. "Sorry. Now I'm really worried."

A white pickup was parked sideways in the lighthouse parking area. As they drove closer, Maggie noticed the passenger door was hanging open. James parked, and leaving his own door open and the headlights on, ran to investigate. Within moments, he put his head inside. "Only one set of footprints. It looks like he's carrying her. Call the police." He ran to the back of the car, opened the trunk, and rummaged around.

Maggie dialed Robert Linton directly, grateful that she had a signal. She couldn't imagine explaining the situation to dispatch, since they hadn't seen any evidence of a crime—yet. To a casual eye, it would look like a romantic rendezvous at the lighthouse.

Robert picked up immediately, for which she was also grateful. He also got the picture right away, especially when she mentioned the white truck. "I'll be right out there along with backup. Be careful, Maggie."

As he said that, James dashed past the car holding a tire iron aloft. It didn't take much imagination to figure out what he planned to do.

"Of course I will." Maggie hung up and got out of the car. She was not going to let James face Tyler Monroe alone.

She found James standing near the lighthouse, scanning the dark, windswept cliffs. Below them, the ocean roared as breakers crashed against the rocks. It was a stormy night, like the one when Sarah and John escaped to Boston. People could disappear on nights like this and it would be called a tragic accident brought on by the weather.

"They're not out here!" James shouted above the wind and waves.

Maggie pointed. "They must be inside."

"You really should wait in the car."

She crossed her arms across her chest and shook her head. "No way. I'm coming with you." She tapped her head with one finger. "Besides, two heads are better than one. We don't have time to argue about this."

He shook his head. "All right. But be careful and let me take the lead."

"Of course."

They ran through the snow, heads bent against the wind and driving flakes.

The lighthouse door was unlocked, and they crept inside, careful to move as quietly as possible so as not to tip off Tyler that they were there. Maggie hovered behind James as he checked the rooms, tire iron held aloft. No one was in the main room or the office or the bedrooms.

That left the tower. They tiptoed up the metal treads, Maggie wincing whenever a footstep clanged, echoing in her ears like a thunderclap. Tonight she was so focused on the goal, on reaching

Mackenzie in time, that the dizzying view down the spiral sweep didn't bother her at all.

At the top, James paused to take a breath. "The moment of truth." He reached for the door latch. "Are you ready?"

"As I'll ever be." Maggie straightened her spine, fists clenched, eager to wrest Mackenzie from Tyler's grasp. She hoped they weren't too late . . .

The room was empty, like the others below.

"Where can they be?" James swung his head back and forth. "Did we miss them outside?"

A movement on the outside deck caught Maggie's eyes. "They're out there!" Shock iced her belly as the lighthouse beam illuminated the scene. Tyler had Mackenzie propped up against the railing, her head lolling. Maggie grabbed James's arm. "He's going to throw her over! What can we do?"

James pointed to the doors leading out to the deck, opposite each other in the circular room. "I'll go out that one on the right and circle around. You go out and distract him."

Now that action was upon her, Maggie panicked. "How?"

His face was grim. "Anything to prevent him from killing her." He reached the door and slipped through.

Maggie watched in horror as Tyler put his arms around Mackenzie's waist and hoisted her up. Was she too late? The sight galvanized her and she bolted across the room and through the door.

"Stop!" she cried.

Tyler jumped in surprise and his arms loosened enough so that Mackenzie slipped back down to the floor of the snow-covered deck. She sat sprawled against the railing, eyes closed.

"What are you doing here?" Tyler's eyes narrowed in anger.

"I'm here to prevent you from making a terrible mistake." Maggie pointed at Mackenzie with a shaking hand. "You don't really want to kill her, do you?"

Tyler glared down at Mackenzie. "Her? She's a nice kid, but—"

"But she's the heir to the Monroe fortune," Maggie finished for him.

His mouth hung open. "How did you find out?"

"The whole world knows, Tyler. So it's too late." She took a gamble. "I guess creeping around my house at night and leaving your nasty little notes didn't do you any good." *Where in the world is James?*

Tyler's mouth stretched in a nasty grin. "In that case, what's to stop me from throwing you over after her?"

Maggie did her best to remain cool. "I'm not drugged. I'll put up a fight. Besides, it won't really look like a suicide with two women gone, now will it?" *James, you'd better hurry!*

"How did you know—"

She smirked at him. "It's obvious you're staging this to look like Mackenzie was following her ancestor's footsteps. That's if it comes out she's related. Otherwise she looks like a flaky artist who couldn't handle the death of her mother."

He took a threatening step toward her, hands outstretched like claws. "You're too smart for your own good," he snarled.

Maggie took a step back, her foot crunching in the crusty snow. "It's not going to work, Tyler. The historical society has proof that Mackenzie is Sarah Monroe's great-great-granddaughter."

"What proof?" He bared his teeth like a wolf.

"Priscilla Allen's diary, which reveals that Sarah married John Floyd. Mackenzie's great-great-grandfather."

"Who the heck is Priscilla Allen?"

"*My* great-grandmother." James appeared behind Tyler and hit him over the head with the tire iron. Tyler staggered and crumpled to the floor, knocked out by the blow.

Maggie's knees gave out, and she leaned against the wall of the lighthouse. "Whew. I thought he was going to kill me too." Blue lights flashed, coloring the falling snow. The police had arrived.

James stepped over Tyler and hugged her fiercely. "I wasn't going to let that happen, believe me." His arms tightened, but then Mackenzie let out a small, plaintive groan. James released Maggie reluctantly. "Let's tend to our heiress."

· · · · · · · · · · · · · · · · ·

Mackenzie's hands shook as she inserted the key into the front door of Monroe Mansion. "I can't believe this is my house now. Well, almost."

"Honestly, it's lucky old Mr. Monroe left that provision in his will," Maggie said. "If he'd just left everything to his cousin, you wouldn't have a chance. That's probably why Tyler was so anxious to get you out of the way." When they had gone to court, Horace Monroe's will had been dug up, and they'd found that he'd left a provision for his daughter.

> *Though I have little hope that it may be so, if my beloved daughter, Sarah, is somehow found alive, the entirety of my estate is to go to her, but for a small sum of $1,000, which will go to my cousin. He shall only inherit on condition that he signs a legal written contract vowing that his will shall have the above provision, and his descendants shall place in their wills the same provision in case Sarah or her descendants are found. If he or any of his descendants refuse, they shall not inherit my estate, and it is to be divided as the court sees fit.*

The historical society had turned out in full force to prove Mackenzie's bloodline, with Priscilla's diary leading the way. The legal system in Boston provided census, birth, and marriage records that helped them trace Mackenzie's family tree. With this and Tyler's confession to attempted murder, a judge had given Mackenzie a provisional right to live at the mansion. The rest of the estate had to go through the formality of probate, and Mackenzie was told that if other living descendants were found, she would probably have to share the estate with them. "I wouldn't mind at all if it meant having more family," she'd confided to Maggie.

"We're thrilled for you, Mackenzie," Ruth said. She and the other members of the historical society stood on the porch, waiting to tour the house.

At the back of the crowd, Ina bobbed up and down, attempting to see around the much taller Daisy. "What's the holdup? Do you need some help up there?"

The key turned with a click. "She's got it, Ina," June said.

The door swung open and Mackenzie stepped inside, the group of ladies crowding in after her. Many "oohs" and "aahs" echoed in the high-ceilinged foyer as they caught glimpses of the mansion's treasures.

"It's like a time capsule that no one has touched for a hundred years," Ruth said.

"Good thing Tyler Monroe didn't have time to get his claws into it," Ina said. "He would've ruined it." She ran one hand along the smoothly polished banister and end finial, a pineapple. "They did nice work back then."

"He was planning to sell a lot of the furniture," Maggie said, "so you're right there, Ina. Carriage House was going to put in a quote."

Mackenzie turned around. "I've been meaning to tell you this, Maggie, but I really don't want to sell anything right now." Her cheeks flushed. "I know you wanted to buy some of the bedroom sets, and I hate to say no, but—"

"Don't worry about it, Mackenzie," Maggie said. "We totally understand." She herself wouldn't part with a single item in

Sedgwick Manor. Every object was connected to family history or had been important to her aunt. The women wandered through the double parlor, dining room, study, butler's pantry, and kitchen. The last was a hulking colossus of a room with tiled walls, a linoleum floor, and fixtures straight out of the early 1900s. There were only a few floor-to-ceiling cabinets and very little counter space. A huge scrubbed worktable dominated the center of the room.

"I might do some work in here," Mackenzie admitted. "I'll need a good kitchen for what I'm planning."

"What's that, Mackenzie?" Liz Young asked. "This reminds me of the rectory kitchen before I got ahold of it."

"I'm turning the house into an artist's retreat. Several times a year, I'll select a group to come here for lessons from top artists, outdoor fun, and plenty of time to work."

"That sounds wonderful," Daisy said. "Somerset Harbor is a perfect spot for artists."

"There's something else I want to tell you all," Mackenzie said. They gathered around to listen. "You have been so wonderful to me, so welcoming. And I know that some of you"—she looked guiltily at Maggie and Fran—"had to endure some really nasty things because of me."

"That was all Tyler Monroe, not your fault," Maggie said firmly. The depth of her relief when she realized Mackenzie wasn't behind the mysterious events had revealed how much she had come to care for the young woman. She still didn't know what Cody had meant by his remarks, and when the time was right, she planned to broach the topic. Not that it really mattered; Mackenzie was the legitimate heir to the Monroe fortune.

"Be that as it may, I'm so, so grateful for your support and help. That's why I'm going to donate the contents of Sarah Monroe's bedroom to the historical society. I figure it will make a nice exhibit."

The women burst into exclamations of thanks and excitement while Mackenzie blushed in pleased embarrassment.

Ina clapped her hands. "We could charge admission and raise money for the lighthouse."

"Great idea, Ina," June said.

"Speaking of the lighthouse, I plan on making a sizable donation once I have access to funds." Mackenzie's blush deepened. "I want to do another matching grant the size of the one you already got."

Maggie was stunned, as were the others. Even Ina only managed a squeak of joy.

"That is extremely generous," Ruth said. "Are you sure?"

"Absolutely. It will be my way of saying thank you. For saving my life, finding my family, and giving me a home." Mackenzie put up one hand. "But enough of that. I'd like to invite you ladies to go through all the cupboards and drawers in the house. I know you're dying to—as I am—and maybe we'll find the quilt blocks and everything else that went missing."

"I sure hope so," Fran said. "I still feel terrible that they were snatched on my watch."

With cries of excitement, the women left the kitchen, except for Liz, who wanted to browse through the kitchen cupboards.

"Do you want to check Sarah's room?" Mackenzie asked Maggie. "Maybe he put them in there."

"I'd love to." Maggie followed Mackenzie upstairs and into the room with its wisteria wallpaper. Everything was the same as when she had last been there.

Mackenzie stood just inside the doorway, a look of awe on her face. "I can't believe this was my great-great-grandmother's bedroom."

"I know the feeling," Maggie said, putting her arm around the younger woman's shoulders. "I experience it every day at the mansion. I love that sense of history, of connection to those who came before me."

Mackenzie wandered to the bureau, where she picked up the silver hand mirror and gazed into its silvery surface. "She used to use this every day, I bet, when she brushed her hair."

Maggie bit her lip, not sure how to broach the subject of Cody's revelations. Maybe she should just let it go. But then she feared there would always be a faint shadow between her and Mackenzie, and she didn't want that. "Mackenzie, I have something to ask you. Cody Becker asked me to come to the jail and—"

Mackenzie set the mirror down and gave her a sharp look. "He didn't try to draw you into his mess, did he?"

"No no. Nothing like that. Well, he wanted me to see if you would talk to him, but I couldn't promise that."

The young woman began to pace around the room, her hands twisting in agitation. "Will I ever be free of that man? He's nothing but trouble."

"Pastor David from the church is working with him to turn his life around," Maggie said. "Let's pray that happens."

Mackenzie stopped in front of the window and twitched aside the lace curtain to look at the ocean view. "I have been. But I still don't want to see him again, ever."

Maggie felt remorseful at bringing up such a sore subject, but she needed to press through to the end. "He did say something odd. He implied that you suspected you might be related to someone wealthy here."

Mackenzie spun around, her cheeks flaming. "I didn't know if I was, but I have to admit I hoped it would be true. I lost my mom and then I felt so lonely for family—any family. So I thought of the photo my mom gave me and decided to look into it." She turned to survey the bedroom. "It was a fun fantasy—hoping I was really the long-lost daughter of a king and queen instead of a café waitress." Her mouth turned down. "I loved my mom, but we were really poor. Third-floor walk-up, beater car, thrift store shopping, the whole bit." She put her hands over her face. "I know, it was really greedy of me, and I feel horrible now that my fantasy has come true."

Maggie moved to stand beside the young woman, who was now crying. She put her arm around her. "Don't. The Monroe fortune is legally yours, and you're already planning to put it to very good use. That's all we can do—use our gifts responsibly. I had to learn the same thing." She confessed her own discomfort over inheriting her aunt's estate.

Mackenzie turned herself into Maggie's arms and sobbed for a few minutes more. Then she pulled away and dried her eyes with a clean tissue Maggie found in her pocket. "Thanks, I think I needed that." Her voice broke again. "I wish my mom was still alive to share in my good fortune."

Maggie squeezed her hand. "I know." She had the same thoughts about her late husband.

Ina burst into the room. "We found the blocks!" she trumpeted. "They were in the kindling box by the living room fireplace."

Maggie gasped. "He was going to burn them? Are they all there?"

"Yes ma'am. All present and accounted for. Fran's looking them over to make sure they're still in good shape."

"I just wish we could find the one made by my great-grandmother," Maggie said. "I don't even know what it depicted."

Mackenzie looked up from the sketchbook, a strange expression on her face. "I think I might know." She dashed downstairs, followed by Ina and Maggie. "Wait here," Mackenzie called as she ran to the front door.

Maggie and Ina joined the others in the dining room, where Fran had laid out the blocks along the table. "They're okay,

Maggie," Fran said as they entered the room. "We also found the photos and newspaper articles—everything that went missing."

"That's a relief."

"A huge relief," Ruth agreed. "Now we can do our exhibit."

The front door opened and slammed shut, and Mackenzie appeared in the dining room doorway, lugging a large duffel bag. She dumped it onto the floor and knelt to unzip the top, then rooted around inside it.

"Here it is." Mackenzie pulled a square pillow out of the bag and presented it to Maggie. "Besides the wedding photo, this is the only thing we had that belonged to my great-great-grandmother."

Maggie took the pillow and stared at its design as the others crowded around to look over her shoulder. In the middle was an appliqued picture of a lighthouse, the Somerset Harbor lighthouse. Maggie's pulse began to race. "Do you think . . .?"

Mackenzie was still rummaging around. "I do." She pulled out a manicure kit and removed the small scissors. "Let's find out." She held her hand out for the pillow.

"Are you sure? I mean, what if we're wrong?" Maggie asked Fran.

"Then we'll stitch it back together," Fran said.

Mackenzie deftly cut the stiches holding the pillow together. Then she removed the stuffing and turned the shell inside out. She handed it to Maggie. "You do the honors."

Maggie gazed down at the pillow. On the reverse of the lighthouse, the writing was still bright and fresh. "*Your friend, Julia Sedgwick, 1898. Remember us,*" she read aloud. Tears sprang to her eyes at the thrill of holding something her great-grandmother had stitched with love.

She turned the case right side out and gently placed it on the table in the center of the other blocks, where it belonged. The women regarded the united pieces silently, one or two wiping away their own tears. Maggie gazed around at their sweet faces.

Sometimes being a friend meant keeping a secret—and sometimes it meant figuring one out. And like the ladies of the quilting guild over a hundred years before, she was blessed, so blessed, with a dear circle of friends.

To discover all that country decorating
has to offer and see the creative home
decorating tips that inspire Maggie and
her friends, check out the latest issue of
Country Sampler at CountrySampler.com!